REFLECTIONS AT MIRROR POND

REFLECTIONS AT MIRROR POND

Geri' Myers Goodwin

JONES MEDIA PUBLISHING

Jones Media Publishing
10645 N. Tatum Blvd. Ste. 200-166
Phoenix, AZ 85028
www.JonesMediaPublishing.com

Disclaimer:

The author strives to be as accurate and complete as possible in the creation of this book, notwithstanding the fact that the author does not warrant or represent at any time that the contents within are accurate due to the rapidly changing nature of the Internet.

While all attempts have been made to verify information provided in this publication, the Author and the Publisher assume no responsibility and are not liable for errors, omissions, or contrary interpretation of the subject matter herein. The Author and Publisher hereby disclaim any liability, loss or damage incurred as a result of the application and utilization, whether directly or indirectly, of any information, suggestion, advice, or procedure in this book. Any perceived slights of specific persons, peoples, or organizations are unintentional.

In practical advice books, like anything else in life, there are no guarantees of income made. Readers are cautioned to rely on their own judgment about their individual circumstances to act accordingly. Readers are responsible for their own actions, choices, and results. This book is not intended for use as a source of legal, business, accounting or financial advice. All readers are advised to seek the services of competent professionals in legal, business, accounting, and finance field.

Printed in the United States of America

ISBN: 978-1-948382-03-8 paperback
JMP2020.3

A special thanks to the City of Bend, Oregon.
Book cover and author bio photo credit belongs to
Nina Montgomery with Montgomery Capture.

CONTENTS

CHAPTER ONE

Mirror Pond

12 years ago -

"Jason, stop playing with those worms and get one on your hook!" Lexi said, shaking her head in irritation. "Here ... hand me your line. I will do it."

Jason dropped the worms into her palm, carefully handing her the hook and line.

"Keep an eye on my pole, Jason. One of us is taking a fish home to Momma today."

He rested his head on his knees, eyes locked on the tip of the pole. If he missed the tug, he would never hear the end of it. "It must hurt, you know, when they bite onto that hook. I don't want to see you thump one in the head after you bring it in, either. It all seems so cruel."

Lexi cast the line, waiting for the sound of the plunk as it landed on the glassy water. She slowly reeled it in just taut enough to feel the tug of a catch. She turned to look at her friend, raising her eyebrow in curiosity. "Jason, what's going on with you? Since when are you such a sissy about fishing?"

He looked down at his fingers covered in mud and worm slime. Lexi waited for his response, but he remained silent. It seemed that in the last year or so, Jason had become more quiet and sensitive. No doubt a direct result of the unfortunate home life he had to endure.

"Well? Do you want to stop fishing now?" she said.

"No. I never said that. Never mind."

The last time Jason reeled in a fish, the hook had gone right through the trout's eyeball. He could not get the vision out of his head. He had tugged, cringing at the sight of the eye stretching with each pull. The dilemma troubled him. He couldn't throw the fish back into the water with a hook stuck in it, but it sickened him to watch it suffer as he tried to retrieve it.

Lexi's dark brown ponytail began to sway, curls popping out around her face from the breeze that had moved in on their day. Mirror Pond had gone from smooth glass to choppy waters in a matter of minutes.

The crackling sound of footsteps on pine needles alerted the young friends that someone was headed their way.

"Hey, you guys, Momma says there is a storm headed our way," said Christopher, Lexi's older brother by a few years. "She sent me down here to fetch you to come on home."

Lexi glanced up at the sky to see dark clouds moving in. "We just got our lines in the water. Give us ten more minutes, please, Chris? The fish always bite better when the sun takes a hike."

Jason stood, brushed off his jeans and began to bring his line in. Pole in hand, he waited for Lexi. His foot tapped with annoying rhythm.

"Go on without me, Jason. I'm a big girl. Been coming out here since birth."

"Jason, just leave her," Christopher said. "Who cares? Let's go! It'll be her behind when she gets back."

Hesitant to leave Lexi alone, Jason rubbed his forehead and slowly turned on his heels, dragging the pole along the dock. Raindrops began to hit the top of his head, and the sound of thunder rolled like an angry beast. The two boys picked up their pace, trying to outrun Mother Nature's pounding tears. With every few steps, Jason looked behind, hoping Lexi had changed her mind. But she was a stubborn girl with a sassy attitude, and he wasn't the least bit surprised she stayed back.

Lexi stood at the foot of the dock feeling conflicted. She'd never liked thunderstorms. The rain felt like hard pellets on her skin and the thunder warned her what was to come next. Just when she was about to throw in the towel and reel the line in, she felt the tug she longed for. With both feet planted firmly on the dock as her elbows dug into her stomach, her hand moved quickly in circles to bring the slippery sucker in.

"Jeez, it's a big one. Ugh ... come on, boy."

Lightning crackled, lighting up the sky as if Hercules were descending. Jason jumped and came to a halt. He twisted his neck to look back toward Mirror Pond.

"Jason, what are you doing?" Christopher said. "Let's keep moving."

"I'm going back for Lexi!" Jason turned, dropping his pole, and ran like a bat out of hell. His clothes began to feel weighted down from being soaked by the pounding rain, inevitably slowing him down. He pushed tree branches aside, nearly tripping over a log. A child's faint scream filtered through the air. Terror flooded his veins, pumping his heart out of his chest.

"Lexi!"

CHAPTER TWO

'It's Alexis'

Present day -

"Alexis ... Alexis ... wake up!"

Her head shot up from the lunch room table as the uninvited interruption jerked her out of some serious REM sleep.

"Are you all right, hon?" Olivia said. "Dr. Peterson's next patient is here. Feisty pup, but cute as all get out."

"Oh, my gosh. Sorry," Lexi said, raising her arms high in an elongated stretch. "I just lay my head down for a second. I'm on my way. Thanks, Olivia."

Gathering her long dark hair together and securing it into a bun high on top of her head, Lexi made her way to the examination room, where a one-year-old black Lab awaited her.

"Oh, no. Looks like somebody tried to get acquainted with a porcupine," Lexi said, gazing at the quills stuck all around his nose. "Ouch, bud. That's got to hurt."

A faint knock at the door diverted her attention.

"Sorry to interrupt, Alexis. Christopher called to remind you of the party tonight for Jason. He said, and I quote, 'Dress like a girl and don't be late.'"

Lexi's brow furrowed as she looked down at her blue scrubs. Olivia's expression was smug as she placed yet another pencil into her blond beehive of a hair do and gently shut the door behind her.

Lexi smiled at the amused dog owner and a faint chuckle came out of her mouth. "My brother. Thinks he is so hilarious. As if I don't know how to dress like a girl."

Growing up, Jason and Christopher referred to Lexi as "one of the guys" on more than one occasion. The thought popped into her mind as she tried to remember how she looked the last time she saw Jason. He had been away at school in Seattle for the past couple of years and didn't venture back home to Bend very often.

Lexi filled out the last of her charts for the day, made sure the back office was spic and span and jetted out of the veterinary office in a hurry. She loved her job as a vet tech, but Christopher lectured her about being married to the profession.

"You need to get out, Lexi," he'd say. "Go on some dates and have fun for God's sake."

Lexi could hear his voice in her head. She knew it was out of love and concern. Their parents had died in a car accident the year of her seventeenth birthday, and her brother had taken over as guardian, effortlessly looking after her. Five years later, they still lived together in their parents' home. Every room was filled with memories that kept them forever bonded to the rustic cabin.

Lexi pulled into the driveway and rushed inside the house to get ready.

"Crap ... I am so late. Crap, crap, *crap!*"

She threw open her closet door, nearly pulling it off its hinges. Her scrubs were off in seconds and thrown into a laundry basket. After grabbing a white blouse and blue skinny jeans, she lay on the bed to allow the tight pants to slide over her hips, kicking her legs back and forth in an effort to get the job done. She sucked in a deep breath while pulling up the zipper and fastening the button. She lay there for a moment, afraid that if she sat up, all would come bursting out the seams. She pushed herself off the bed, legs stiff and straight like Frankenstein's.

One wrong move tonight and I will be exposing more than I care to, she thought.

Her five-foot-ten frame never stopped her from wearing high heels when she wanted to. After plucking a pair of nude stilettos from the tidy shoe rack in her closet, she shot to the bathroom to freshen up. Her long wavy dark brown tendrils often looked like an out-of-control mess. Scavenging through her hair products, she grabbed a bottle and squirted a glob of goo into her palm. After rubbing her hands together to emulsify the cream, she applied it evenly to her locks.

She debated tucking the blouse into her jeans and decided there was absolutely no room. She tied a knot in the blouse above her stomach and rolled the sleeves up just above her wrists. After careful inspection, she made the decision to unfasten one more button from the top for a softer, sexier look. Lexi didn't always exude a delicate, gentle personality. She often rubbed people the wrong way. Not because she wasn't friendly—because she didn't take crap from anyone.

Just when she was about to grab her car keys and go, her cell phone blasted, causing her to jump.

"Great. I bet I know who that is." She answered it. "Hey, Christopher. I'm on my way. Be there in five." She hung up in the middle of his ranting, rushing out the front door to her black Jeep Wrangler. She tossed her purse into the passenger seat and with one swift move started the engine. As she peeled out of the driveway, she tried to fasten her seat belt. She'd barely gained momentum when the traffic reared its ugly head.

"Of course! I am going to hit every stop light in town."

Blowing out a breath of frustration, Lexi closed her eyes to count to ten. The nervous tension felt hard to tame. It wasn't about traffic or being late. It was all about seeing Jason. Her right hand left the steering wheel to massage the butterflies swirling in her stomach.

The driveway to the pub came into sight. Lexi took the turn a bit prematurely, jumping the curve. Dust and dirt clouded up behind the Jeep as she pulled into the closest parking spot. In her rush, she slammed the car door shut on her purse strap and the strap acted as a rubber band, jerking her backward. Feeling embarrassed and clumsy, she looked around the parking lot to see if anyone had witnessed the careless act. She quickly fumbled for her keys to unlock the door and release the strap from captivity.

Good Lord, just slow down, Lexi. Pull yourself together.

She shook her arms vigorously to release the anxiety flowing through her system. With focus and determination, she made her way into the pub.

The first thing to hit her senses was the sound of voices muddled by loud music. It was a full house. Lexi scanned over heads and bodies to look for Jason and Christopher. Couples were tearing up the dance floor to the sound of Keith Urban blaring from the jukebox. No sign of the boys. Her stiletto's clicked on the hard wood floor as she made her way to the back patio. She paused in the doorway, careful not to get her heels stuck in the metal grooves. Feeling flushed from nerves and anxiety, she welcomed the cool air blowing directly on her from a nearby ceiling fan. She noticed a group huddled together and looking out over the Deschutes River. It had to be Jason and Christopher's entourage. She caught Jason's eye, blocking out everything else around him. A tender, faint smile surfaced in the corner of his mouth.

"Hey, Lexi! Over here!" Christopher yelled, arms waving in the air.

He stood shorter than Jason, with a stocky build from working out and dark brown hair shaved into a tight fade.

Jason swallowed the lump in his throat and proceeded to flush it down with beer. Christopher slapped him on the back and smiled.

"The family is all together now."

Right … family, Jason thought. He'd spent more time with the Taylor family than his own over the years. When Mr. and Mrs. Taylor passed away, he moved in with Christopher and Lexi to help out. It had also been a move to save himself from the darkness of the walls surrounding his own home.

Waving back in acknowledgment, Lexi made her way through corn hole games and fire pits. Jason overheard some of the fellows talking.

"Man, Christopher's baby sis is looking damn fine."

Jason did not welcome the sound of that one bit. He turned to see which one of their friends had made the comment. They all saw the intense look in his eyes, warning them. Knowing it was in their best interest to change the subject, they turned around to shoot the shit about sports.

"Hey, Jason," Lexi said, standing on her tiptoes to hug him. Closing her eyes, she took in his familiar scent, reminding her of cedar and spice. The feeling of his arms around her encouraged her to step closer into the embrace. He had plentiful light brown hair that curled at the ends when it was long. The kind of hair a woman loved to run her fingers through. She stepped out of the embrace to look into his blue eyes. His six-foot frame with broad shoulders made her feel surrounded by masculinity.

"Congratulations, Jason. We are so proud of you. And you already have a job lined up. That is amazing."

An unfamiliar gentleman approached, interrupting the sentimental reunion.

"Pardon me, but it looks like we haven't met yet," the stranger said, completely intrigued by Lexi.

Jason smiled apologetically at her, annoyed by the disruption. "Lexi, this is my new boss, Gage. He owns the engineering company I am going to work for. I start on Monday."

"Hello, Gage. Nice to meet you. I actually go by Alexis." She offered her hand.

Jason's eyes narrowed.

"Since when, Lexi?" he said, laughing as if it were ridiculous.

"There is quite a lot you don't know about me anymore, Jason," she said, her right hand resting firmly on her hip. She cocked her head, waiting for a response.

Uh-oh, Gage thought, slowly stepping away from the scene that was about to unfold. Jason and Lexi were oblivious to his absence.

"Well, you've still got that fire in you, I see. That hasn't changed, A-lex-is! Do you still carry a Glock in your back pocket wherever you go, too?" He reached for the back pocket of her jeans, searching for the dark metal pistol. His head moved in close to hers and she could feel the touch of his hands.

"Hey! Back off, Jason. What the hell are you doing?" She reached out her arm to shove him away.

"What? No Glock? You have got to be kidding me." He laughed, trying to have fun play with Lexi, patting her down like a criminal.

"I left the Glock in my car, okay? It seemed a little much to bring it into your party."

"Mm-hmm. I knew it, Lexi Jane."

Lexi's face softened and their eyes locked. Jason was the only person who'd ever used her middle name, most commonly when he was teasing her. She found it endearing and always loved it. She couldn't remember the last time he called her that. Clearing her throat, she broke the trance to speak.

"So, are you moving back in with us now that you are back? Your room is exactly the same. We haven't touched anything. It is always yours, Jason."

"I already talked it over with Chris. I assumed he cleared it with you. After the party tonight, I'm moving back in."

Lexi smiled, her heart racing with excitement. The day Jason left for college had been another loss and heartbreak for her. They grew up together, supported each other through all the hard times. Having him back home was a dream come true.

"All right then. Guess I will see you back home. Enjoy the rest of the night, Jason." She inched away to leave the pub.

"Are you leaving already? Come on, stay a while longer."

Right at that moment, a tall blond with seduction written all over her face strolled up behind Jason and looped her arm around his. Her lips went straight for his ear as she leaned in to whisper.

"Hey, Jason, I have been waiting very patiently to dance with you," she said.

Lexi looked straight into her eyes and smirked. Annalise— once again. The thorn in her side all through high school and beyond.

Damn it.

"Hey, Annalise. I was just heading out. See you later, Jason."

Lexi waved good-bye to him like a cocky drill sergeant.

"Don't wait up for him, Lexi," Annalise said, a seductive grin implying she would be taking care of him for the rest of the night.

Lexi got into her jeep, slammed the door shut and squeezed the steering wheel so tight her fingers turned blood red.

"Ugh ... that girl burns me up! Why? Why do I let her do that to me?"

Forcing her fingers to release the steering wheel, she stretched each one out so she could start the car and leave. Dust flew like the Tasmanian Devil as she sped out of the parking lot.

She pulled into the driveway of her house, turned off the engine and tossed her keys into her purse. She removed the Glock from the glove box and carried it safely into the house. She was greeted by two happily wagging tails and wet tongues.

"Hey, buddies!" she said, bending down to pet her loyal pals.

Christopher had adopted a golden mix from the pound for Lexi not long after their parents passed away. She named her Sadie. A few years later, after Lexi started working for the vet clinic, she brought home a black Lab mix named Stout. The day she walked into the house snuggling a calico kitten, Christopher put his foot down.

"No more pets, Lexi."

He loved her passion for animals. A bit of an introvert, she had always been more comfortable around animals than around people. He knew they filled a void in her life, but enough was enough.

Sadie and Stout followed Lexi into her bedroom and sat patiently while she changed into white cotton shorts and a black tank top. After locking up the Glock, she proceeded to slip on a pair of black sandals, grab two dog leashes and escort Sadie and Stout out for a walk. They shuffled out the back door, down the steps and through the woods. The moon was full and bright, the perfect flashlight. They headed straight for Mirror Pond. The air was unusually still. Not a single branch stirred throughout the thickness of trees. The silence felt eerie and Lexi knew that if she were to scream, she could be heard for miles. She bent down to remove the dogs' leashes, allowing them to roam free. Lexi walked out onto the dock, slipped off her sandals and dipped her feet into the chilly pond. The glassy water reflected the moon like a mirror, leaving her mesmerized. This was exactly what she needed. Annalise had thrown a lit match right into her soul, burning her up inside and out. Deciding to bring her anger down a notch, she stripped down to bare skin and plunged into the pond. Sadie and Stout followed without hesitation. When Lexi resurfaced, a few choice words came flying out of her mouth.

"Holy Mother of ... the water is freezing cold. It is way too soon for skinny-dipping."

She looked over at Sadie and Stout, who had already climbed out of the pond. Their collars jingled as they vigorously shook the water out of their fur. Stout paused, growling as the fur rose on his back. They were no longer alone at Mirror Pond.

Chapter Three

Shattered Memories

Sadie and Stout stood their ground, ready to protect. Lexi swam closer to the dock and hid underneath, keeping watch for the intruder. Her lips quivered as she focused on being silent. The dogs took off, tails wagging. Out of the darkness of the trees, standing right under the moonlight, was Jason.

"Jason? Jason, you scared the living crap out of me!!" Lexi yelled.

He got down on one knee to pet Sadie and Stout, who were ever so pleased with his presence. Grinning, he stood and walked closer to the edge of the pond. He began unbuttoning his plaid shirt, removing it casually. Lexi swam out from under the dock.

"What are you doing?" she said nervously.

"What does it look like I am doing? I'm taking my clothes off to join you. We used to do this together all the time. Is there a problem?"

Lexi quickly turned her head in the opposite direction as he began pulling off his blue jeans.

"Um, no. No problem. I just don't think—"

Jason dived into the water, creating a slight wake. The water splashed her, and her eyes grew big as he swam straight for her. Surfacing beside her, he wiped the water from his blue eyes and smiled.

"Man, this feels great. We haven't done this in a long time, Lexi Jane. I'm surprised you even got in since it's not the middle of summer yet."

"Yeah, well, here I am. Swimming in the pond. With you. You know, we are going to freeze our asses off when we get out."

Jason laughed.

They swam in small circles around each other. Lexi could feel his leg brush against hers, making her tingle inside.

"So, what happened to Annalise?" she said.

Jason raised his eyebrows. "Do I see fire in those hazel eyes? Yep, definitely. Burning like an inferno, I'd say."

Lexi pursed her lips as she splashed water into his face. He grabbed her arms tight, pulling her close to his chest. She stared him down, determined not to look away. Their arms were the only barrier keeping her breasts from rubbing against him. The moment he loosened his grip, she pushed back, breaking free.

"You didn't answer my question, Jason," she said.

Trying to allow distance between them, Lexi dog-paddled in the opposite direction as she awaited his answer. He followed in attempt to be playful. The closer he got, the more nervous she felt. Jason could sense her unease. He smiled at the accomplishment.

"I introduced Annalise to Gage, then slipped out of the pub before she could notice. I imagine he will be stuck with her for the rest of the night. He is either going to be pissed as hell at me on Monday morning or thanking me profusely. Hard to say."

Lexi laughed. "I hope he keeps her indefinitely."

Jason shook his head. "You are so bad, Lexi."

She swam back up to the dock and paused at the ladder.

"I am going to get out now."

Jason smiled, slowly turning around to swim back to the other side of the pond, where he'd left his clothes. Lexi quickly climbed the ladder, covered her chest with her arms and snatched up her clothes. Shivering and covered in goose bumps, her teeth chattered as she tried to get her shorts and shirt back on. She followed Sadie and Stout toward Jason.

Through the moonlight, Lexi caught a glimpse of his naked butt as he struggled to get his jeans on over his wet skin. They walked back up to the house together, enjoying the beautiful night. The act felt so natural, even in silence. When they entered the house, it was dark and quiet. Christopher had not yet returned home. Lexi and Jason were alone. The calm inside her turned to jitters. She headed straight for her bedroom, shut the door and leaned against it as if protecting herself from someone. Her breathing was heavy and her hand rested across her heart. Being alone with Jason had her all worked up. She ran into the bathroom and started a warm shower. Steam began to fill the room as she removed her clothes. Once inside the shower stall, the water pressure pounding her skin helped to relieve the tension in her body. Rubbing her hands over her face, she wondered why she felt so flustered around Jason. They'd grown up together and knew each other better than anyone else. A memory shot through her mind, taking her back four years. Right before Jason left for college, Christopher threw him a big going-away bash. It was a night that opened the door to a pivotal moment in her life.

* * *

"Lexi, can you go down to the basement and grab some more beer?" Christopher had yelled from the patio, trying to be heard over loud music and chatter.

"Okay. Sure thing."

She weaved in and out of the crowd of people in the kitchen to find her way to the basement door. After flipping on the light switch, she made her way down the old, rickety wooden stairs. She pulled the refrigerator door open, causing beer bottles to tumble inside the door. She stuck her head inside, inspecting all the options. The music from upstairs created a throbbing vibration she was sure would shake the ceiling. The sound of footsteps descending the stairway caught her attention.

"Chris, I've got this," she said, rolling her eyes. "You didn't need to follow me down here."

Jason stood behind Lexi, shaking his head at her sass. Her long dark hair fell to one side, the ends feathering across her breast as she remained bending over. He couldn't help but admire her from hip to toe. She wore white shorts that exposed her butt cheeks just enough to be tempting and drive a man crazy. His eyes continued to examine every inch, all the way down her legs. Lexi was no longer the tough tomboy he'd grown up with. She was 100 percent female. The realization made him smile and made him a bit concerned at the same time. He rested his arm across the top of the refrigerator door.

"Lexi ..."

Surprised by the sound of his voice, she quickly raised her head and bumped it against the bottom of the freezer.

"Ouch! Jason, what the ..." she said as she backed herself out of the refrigerator. She held the top of her head and turned to face him.

"I'm so sorry, Lexi," Jason said, trying to stifle his laughter. "I didn't mean to scare you."

"Forget it. You know what I found in here, Jason?" She slowly pulled out a fancy-looking black bottle. The top was wrapped in foil, which was always a very good sign.

"Champagne," he said. "That is the champagne that we have been hoarding in here for so long. I completely forgot about it. Open that puppy up!"

Lexi grabbed a case of beer and handed it to Jason.

"Run this up to Chris, then hurry back. I'm not sharing the bubbles with everyone up there."

He took off up the stairs as she foraged around the basement for some spare glasses. After finding two glass jars, she used the hem of her blue shirt to wipe out any dust from the inside.

"These will do."

She began to remove the foil and untwist the wire when she heard Jason shut the basement door and run down the stairs. She put the bottle between her legs and gripped the cork tight, pulling until it popped free. She filled the two glasses and handed one to Jason.

"Here's to you, Jason. I can't believe you are heading off to college. We are so proud of you." She held her glass high.

"Thank you, Lexi," he said, clicking his glass against hers.

After a few sips, she looked him square in the eyes and spoke softly.

"I'm really going to miss you."

He saw a sadness in her hazel eyes. The last time she looked at him that way, her parents had just died. It wasn't a feeling of guilt that had him torn up. It was desire. His hand came up to grab the side of her head. His eyes left hers, focusing intently on her mouth. The need to kiss her overcame the fear of the consequences. He bent his head to reach her, placing a gentle kiss on her lips. Another kiss, more pressure. Lexi set her glass down and grabbed his waist, gripping the loops of his jeans. His hands came down to grab her buttocks and lift her up to sit on top of the laundry-folding table. She spread her legs so he could step in and get close. He grabbed her legs and wrapped them around his waist. His mouth dived back in for more. They tasted each other with their tongues as their hands began to explore. Jason lifted the hem of her shirt, finding his way underneath. He stroked her bare back, the feel of her bra tempting him to unsnap it. Lexi squeezed her legs tighter, pulling him in closer. Her hands raked the curls in his hair. Her invitation was clear. Jason's erection was getting bigger by the second. Control was slipping away with each kiss and touch and he unhooked her bra. Her breasts exposed and ready for his touch, her body began to tremble, causing Jason to pause. If he wasn't careful, he would take things too far. His mind began attacking his morals. He pulled away from Lexi to slow down. His breathing heavy, he looked into her eyes.

"Lexi, have you ever been touched before?"

Continuing to tremble, she shook her head. "No." she whispered shyly.

Jason stroked the side of her head as he leaned in to kiss her forehead.

"Lexi, we have to stop. I don't want to, but we can't let things go too far. I'm about to have you right here, right now. You're trembling." He held her face in his hands, his eyes pleading for forgiveness. "Lexi, Christopher would never forgive me. He is my best friend, my brother. And you ..."

Lexi pushed him away as she jumped off the table.

"Jason, don't you dare tell me that I am like a sister to you."

Tears filled her eyes as she tried to maintain strength and control. She fumbled with her bra, trying to secure it. Her hands moved to her hips as she braced herself against the crumble of heartache.

"All these years growing up together, you have been like a sister to me, Lexi. But I see a whole different you now. It scares me."

"Jason, I ..." She tried to find the courage to tell him she had been in love with him for as long as she could remember. She'd never dreamed he would ever feel the same way. Her arms fell from her hips in defeat. The chatter in her mind told her what a coward she was as she lied directly to his face. "You are right, Jason. This is crazy. What were we thinking, huh? I mean, you are leaving for college and there is no point getting Christopher all worked up. The champagne got to us. Simple as that. Let's just forget this whole thing ever happened."

"Lexi ..." Jason knew that he'd hurt her and that she was doing some heroic backpedaling.

"Come on. Let's grab our champagne and head back up to the party." She took her glass and bolted up the stairs.

Jason didn't move as he watched her disappear. "Damn it!" he said, pounding his fist against the concrete wall. He slammed what was left of his champagne and grabbed the crotch of his pants to reposition the package in an effort to hide his erection.

When he came out of the basement, he ran into a girl he knew all too well from high school. She was a blond, blue-eyed vixen ready to pounce on Jason's vulnerabilities. He grabbed her hand and they disappeared, not to be seen again for the rest of the night.

The next morning, Lexi woke up debating whether to sleep in or face the day. She lay there, staring at the ceiling and thinking about the huge mess in the house awaiting her. Both hands came up to suppress the throbbing headache punishing her for overindulgence.

"I literally feel like crawling to the bathroom right now," she groaned to herself.

Pathetically dragging herself, she tapped into the medicine cabinet and popped the cap off the bottle of ibuprofen. She dropped three tablets into the palm of her hand and tossed them into her mouth. After swallowing them, she took another large gulp of water and swished it around her mouth to alleviate her cottonmouth.

"I think something died in there last night. Yuck." She stared at her haggard reflection in the bathroom mirror. She picked up her toothbrush, placed an abundance of toothpaste on it and began brushing vigorously. She held her hair back to spit and began a conversation with herself.

"Those guys are not getting out of helping me clean. I am waking their butts up."

She went for Jason's bedroom door first and pounded it with her fist.

Bang, bang, bang.

"Jason! Time to get up!"

She heard footsteps, then the rattling of the door handle. She laughed, knowing that he was without a doubt hungover as hell and ready to let her have it. When the door cracked open, a woman with tousled blond hair and a sheet draped around her like a cloak stood before her.

"Hey, Lexi," the blond said, yawning in her face.

Lexi's eyes popped open wide in shock and anger. "Annalise?"

"As you can see, Jason is unavailable right now. We had a long night." She smiled, suggestively.

Lexi pushed the door open farther to see Jason passed out in his bed.

"Do you mind?" Annalise said, forcing Lexi back into the hallway as she closed the door.

Lexi turned on her heels fuming. Tears poured down her face like a dam that had unexpectedly burst. She took off running to the only place that offered solace. Mirror Pond.

* * *

The shower water turned cold, snapping Lexi's thoughts back to the present. She had drifted off to a place of heartache. After turning off the water, she stepped out of the shower stall and wrapped a white towel around her head and another around her body.

"Lexi, can you come here, please?" Jason called from across the hall.

The tone of his voice was not one of pleasantry. When she reached his room, he was standing in the doorway holding a black duffel bag.

"What? What is it?" she said, concerned.

"Lexi Jane, what is *that* on my bed?"

She smiled like a proud mother and ran over to sit on his bed.

"Jason, this is Patches. The sweetest calico kitty ever."

"Well, I can see that it is a cat, Lexi, but why is it on *my* bed?"

"She loves your bed and she will make a great snuggler, too."

Annoyed, Jason threw his duffel bag on the ground. He folded his arms across his chest, glaring at her with disapproval.

"What is wrong with you, Jason? You love animals."

"It is like Animal Kingdom around here, Lexi."

She stood in front of him. "Well, I suggest you adjust your attitude if you don't want cat pee all over your clothes. Cats are very intuitive, you know?" She cocked her head just enough to cause the bath towel to nearly slide off her head. Readjusting the terry towel more securely, she stomped to the bedroom door and stopped. "Welcome home, Jason."

"Some things never change. You still need a good swat from time to time. Don't think for a second that I am going to start calling you, Alexis."

When she reached her bedroom, she turned to sneer at Jason and slammed the door shut.

Boom!

Jason bent down to pick up his duffel bag, realizing she hadn't taken the cat with her.

"Lexi, damn it!"

CHAPTER FOUR

The Conflict

Jason tossed and turned. His brain had taken over and he was unable to override the uninvited thoughts. Lexi had a way of burning him up inside. Her sultry sass was poison and he wanted desperately to drink it despite the consequences. Furiously sitting up in bed, he tore at his face with his hands to stop the images in his head. The feel of a soft feather brushed against his arm. Drawing his hands away from his face, he saw a pair of glowing amber eyes staring at him. Patches began kneading her sharp nails into his blanket, preparing to settle in.

"No. I do not sleep with cats. You can't stay here."

Patches purred, curling up against Jason. He lay back down, annoyed at the thought of a cat on his bed. Before long, sleep defeated the brain and Jason did in fact, sleep with a cat.

The next morning, Jason awakened to commotion in the house. He picked up Patches, opened the bedroom door and headed toward the living room. Tossing the cat onto the couch, Jason turned around to find Christopher stacking two duffel bags by the front door.

"Hey, man, what's going on?" Jason said.

"Good morning. I'm working out of town this week. Thought I would head out today instead of fighting the traffic in the morning."

Jason followed him into the kitchen, where Christopher poured two mugs of black coffee.

"What do you mean you are working out of town?" Jason said nervously. "Why, what for?"

Steam created a small pool of sweat on Christopher's forehead as he sipped his coffee. His brow furrowed as he tried to decipher Jason's troubled reaction.

"I do own a construction business and occasionally I work out of town. What is the problem, Jason? Lexi will be here. Do you need a night light in your room or what?"

"Ha ha ha, very funny. It's just, well, I just got home and now you are leaving?" Jason blew out a breath and ran his hand through his hair.

There was no way he could tell Christopher that he was nervous about being home alone with Lexi all week. This was bad ... real bad.

"I know what this is, Jason. You are worried about your first day on the job tomorrow. Look man, you've got this." Chris set his coffee mug on the counter, walked over to Jason and gave him a big slap on the back.

"I will see you guys at the end of the week."

Christopher picked up his duffel bags and was out the door before Jason could protest.

Lexi surprised Jason by coming into the house through the back door. Sadie and Stout forcefully nudged themselves in front of her to get to Jason first. Tails wagging, he bent down and stroked their fur.

"It is gorgeous out," Lexi said. "We had a great hike. How are you this morning?" She filled a glass of water from the kitchen sink.

She gulped it down so fast that water leaked around the glass and down her chest. She wiped her lips with the back of her hand.

Jason stared as she stood before him with sexy tousled hair and nipples erect against her white tank top.

"What? Are you still sore with me from last night? Come on. It was like old times, right?" She smiled.

Jason stood and cleared his throat. "Right. Just like old times."

"What would you like to do today? We could drive up to the Crooked River for a picnic and fly-fishing. Your waders should still be here somewhere. Probably the basement. Or we could spend the day playing cornhole and drinking beer at the brew pub." She was talking ten miles a minute. "Whatever we do, I hope you don't mind if we take Sadie and Stout. Jason? Are you listening to anything I am saying?"

"Shower ... I need a shower."

"O-kay. By all means, go take a shower."

As he took off down the hall to his bedroom, she shook her head wondering what had gotten into him.

"Lexi Jane! Come get Patches out of my room ... Now!"

She rolled her eyes and took her time strolling down the hall to retrieve Patches. She stood in the doorway of Jason's room and folded her arms across her chest. "Someone woke up on the wrong side of the bed today."

She had no idea.

She walked past Jason to pick up the lazy calico feline. She rubbed the top of Patches's head wondering how Jason could be so uninterested.

"Look, Jason, if you are not in the mood to do anything together today, it is no problem. I guess I was being presumptuous. It seems you may need some time to yourself today."

The sound of disappointment in her voice tore him up. He wanted nothing more than to spend the day with her. Lexi left his bedroom, gently shutting the door behind her.

"Shit," Jason murmured.

He stormed into the bathroom and started the shower, turning the temperature up as high as it would go, thinking that the feel of the burn would punish him, knowing very well he deserved it. He tore his clothes off and left them in a pile on the floor. His body reacted to the pain, jerking to get away from the hot water pelting his skin and turning it bright red. His mood dark and sullen, he decided it would be the perfect day to visit his childhood home. He hadn't gone back for several years and hadn't really intended to. Until today.

He hoped to escape the house without running into Lexi. He'd hurt her, which was something he seemed to be good at. Avoiding the issue was all could he muster. After climbing into his white Ford-F150, he turned the key to fire up the engine. The exhaust rumbled, giving him away.

Lexi walked to her bedroom window, discreetly pulling a small portion of the curtain aside. She watched as Jason backed out of the driveway and headed down the street, wheels tearing up the road. To where, she didn't know. He wasn't himself. What was going on with him?

Jason drove past his childhood home, not recognizing it. After turning the truck around, he pulled up across the street and parked. He was shocked at what he saw. The vision in front of him was what he had always dreamed of as a child. He stroked his chin, remembering what it had really been like.

* * *

Billy Walker sat in his brown leather recliner, rocking back and forth, staring at the television. The antenna was old, leaving the screen with fuzzy images. Jason stood in the hallway watching him. Billy Walker's eyes were blue like his son's but over time had turned to slate. Not long ago, out of the blue, Jason's mother left, never to be heard from again. They both suffered broken hearts, but his father's would never mend, causing an aftermath that would inevitably cause Jason to lose him as well.

Jason's attention became distracted by a tapping at his bedroom window. Lexi Jane Taylor stood outside the window waving him over. Her ponytail bounced with the gesture, a smile from ear to ear. Jason lifted the window to find her nose nearly pressed to the screen.

"Come on, Jason. I will walk over to Mirror Pond with you."

Over the years, the Walkers and the Taylors had imprinted their own private trail from their houses to the pond. The forest, thick with trees, was no barrier for the threesome. She looked past Jason to see his dad sitting in his recliner looking hypnotized. Lexi's face fell at the despairing sight. Lately, she had been avoiding going inside the house. It was an environment of desolation.

"Yeah ... I'll meet ya out back," Jason said. He closed the window and put on a baseball cap. "I'm heading out, Dad."

He paused for a response. Nothing. He could stay out all day and all night without his father noticing his absence. He took note of the condition of the house before he walked out the door. When his mother left, the personal touches and cheer had gone with her. There wasn't a speck of color or flare. Bare walls, an empty refrigerator and cobwebs were all that remained. Jason ran around to the back of the house to find Lexi pacing back and forth.

"Finally," she said. "Christopher is waiting for us. Let's go."

She grabbed Jason's hand and they ran through the forest. It was the beginning of fall. Clouds hovered above, bringing out the changing colors of the leaves. Lexi stopped short to hide behind a tree. Dropping his hand, she drew her index finger up to her lips.

"Shh ... Check out old man Johnson's backyard. He's been raking leaves. Two beautiful piles just waiting for us, Jason."

"Lexi, no way. He will know it was us."

Her smile grew wide. "I am going for it!"

She sprinted toward Mr. Johnson's backyard. After carefully climbing through the barbed-wire fence, she headed straight for the pile of leaves. One, two, three ... *poof!* Jason watched from behind the tree as she disappeared into the crunchy pillow, leaves billowing into the air. Her arms were the first to surface, then her upper body. She was laughing, staring up at the sky in wonder. Jason watched, mesmerized by her lack of inhibition.

"Lexi Jane Taylor!" a loud voice yelled from the house. "I know that is you out there."

"Oh, crap," she said.

In a flash, she was up off the ground running toward Jason. He had a head start on her. She caught up to him feeling pleased with herself.

"Your papa is going to have your hide, Lexi."

"Maybe," she said, grinning mischievously as if it were totally worth it.

They reached the pond to find fishing poles, worms and snacks on the dock. Christopher had given up on waiting for them and headed back home. Lexi looked at Jason, raising her hand to her hip.

"Today is the day I catch the biggest trout you have ever seen, Jason Walker."

Mother Nature had plans of her own.

CHAPTER FIVE

Let It Go

Jason stared at his childhood home, admiring how it stood out as a bright light in the neighborhood. The home had gone into foreclosure, forcing his dad to move out not long after Jason moved in with the Taylors. He hadn't seen or heard from his dad since. The previously run-down home had fresh yellow paint with white trim and a bright red front door. A beautiful wreath of dried flowers hung on the door, and a mat on the ground read "Happiness Lives Here." He closed his eyes and swallowed. The happiest times of his life were spent at the Taylor house, where love and affection had been in abundance. Safety, hot meals and smiles were a constant. The exact opposite of what was to be found in the Walker house. He wondered why he lacked compassion for his father. He'd probably done the best he could given the circumstances. Smiling at the current sight of the house now, he felt truly pleased that someone had found happiness in that home. He was ready to put a lid on the old memories, sealing them away forever.

He started his truck and let it idle for a few moments before slowly driving away. Relief flooded his veins as he said good-bye to the past. A place he never wanted to visit again.

Lexi was on her hands and knees in front of the fireplace scooping ashes. She worked intently, thankful for the distraction.

"*Cuh, cuh, cuh,*" she coughed as ashes filled the air.

She paused, rubbing the back of her hand across her forehead. Sadie on the left and Stout on the right licked the sides of her face, tails wagging happily.

"You guys, I can't work like this," she said, laughing. "Go on now."

The sound of Jason's pickup truck alerted the pups and they headed for the front door. Lexi continued her work, prepared to give him the silent treatment. She heard him walk in the door and the dogs went nuts. He looked over to see what Lexi was up to and a smile curled the corner of his mouth. She wore a pile of hair in a bun on top of her head and used a black bandanna as a head band to prevent any tendrils from escaping. After dropping the last dustpan's worth of ash into the garbage, she set the garbage can aside and placed six tapered flickering LED candles inside the fireplace for the summer season. Ignoring Jason, she removed her gloves and used the tiny remote to turn them on.

Jason slowly walked over to her. She could sense he was right behind her. She looked up at the ceiling, pondering what to do.

"Lexi ..." he whispered.

The soft tone in his voice settled her down, shifting her attitude in the process. She turned to face him, offering a gentle smile. Her nose and cheeks were covered in soot, and it was all Jason could do not to laugh. He licked the pad of his thumb and reached out to her face. Lexi's brows furrowed.

"Jason?"

He began cleansing her skin, licking his thumb a few more times to get the job done. He wore a cocky smile, but it was his blue eyes staring down into hers that made her heart race. She swallowed, studying him closely.

"There we go," he said. "Much better."

They stood in front of the fireplace quietly staring at each other. Lexi broke the silence, her expression tender.

"Jason, what is going on with you? What did I do?"

His hands came up to embrace her face. He stroked her cheeks with his thumbs, and his mouth came down on hers, kissing her gently. Lexi's hands latched on to his forearms as he came back in for more. More pressure, more urgency. She let go, wrapping her arms around his waist and working her hands up his back. She couldn't get close enough. Jason's tongue took hers, and his hands had found their way to the hem of her T-shirt. He broke off the kiss to remove her shirt over her head and dropped it onto the floor. She wore a black bra with a band of lace just below her breasts. He could see the rise and fall of her chest as she breathed deeply with desire. Lexi shivered with goose bumps as his fingers stroked the sides of her arms. Jason dived into the side of her neck close to her ear with his mouth. She could feel his breath and more shivers erupted. They moved in sync with one another toward the couch. Jason kicked off his shoes and maneuvered

Lexi onto the couch as he hovered above her. She adjusted her legs and hips so that his pelvic area could settle in against hers. It came all too naturally to raise herself up against him, nearly doing him in.

"God, Lexi" he moaned.

His hand massaged her breast. The lace teased him, only allowing a hint of her areola. His fingers moved the material aside to offer him a look. Fascinated by the shape and color, his mouth came down to suck on her nipple. Lexi rubbed his lower back, working her way inside his jeans. He reached down to unsnap his pants for easier access. She felt the soft cotton of his briefs and found the courage to explore under the next layer. The feel of his bare butt excited her. Smooth skin, firm muscle. If it weren't for the barriers of their jeans, he would be inside her.

Caution lights began to blink inside his head. They were headed for danger and fast. He wanted to treat Lexi with respect, and screwing her on the living room couch wouldn't cut it. He kissed her on the forehead and looked into her eyes. The amber around the edges of her irises mirrored burning flames. Lexi's chest lifted with each deep, exhilarated breath.

"What is it? Why did you stop?" she asked, worried about the concerned look in his eyes.

"Lexi, I always feel like I have to fight this ... this feeling and desire I have for you. It's so damn frustrating."

He ran his fingers through his hair and looked up as if asking God why. Why did it have to be this way?

Lexi lay quietly, trying desperately to be patient. "Jason. It's okay. I want this. Please, don't stop."

All of a sudden, there was a forceful banging at the front door, causing both Lexi and Jason to jump.

"Jeez ... are you kidding me?" Lexi said, her heart pounding. "Just don't answer it. Please, Jason."

Sadie and Stout barked and barked, creating more chaos.

Bang bang bang!!

"Shit. I will get it." Jason hopped off the couch, buttoning his pants.

"Wait, Jason ... My shirt ... over there."

Jason picked Lexi's shirt up off the floor and tossed it to her. Scrambling to get it on quickly, she scooted off the couch and headed for the kitchen.

Jason opened the door to an unwanted visitor. *Oh, no. This is bad. Very, very bad.*

"Hey, Jason. You sneaked out on me last night, so I decided to pay you a little visit. Aren't you going to invite me in?" Annalise looked over his shoulder to see if he was alone.

Lexi paced the kitchen floor, her hands digging into her hips. The voice of Annalise made her skin crawl. That pouty, ridiculous voice.

She's like an STD. She disappears for a bit, but always shows up again.

Annalise raised her hand to play with his hair. "Come on, Jason. We have a lot of catching up to do."

She forced her way past him, walking right into the living room. Lexi heard her enter and was completely perplexed. Jason never had any spine when it came to Annalise and she couldn't take it. She took off out the back door, Sadie and Stout following behind.

"Oh, was that Lexi that just left? Hope I wasn't intruding or anything," Annalise said, lying through her teeth.

Her long blond hair lay seductively over her breasts. Not a single strand out of place. Her makeup was done to perfection, as if she were off to the Oscars. Carrying a handbag over her wrist, she casually dropped it onto the dining room table. Jason could not help but notice the cleavage spilling from her shirt, breasts ready to burst out at any moment.

"Actually, Annalise, this is not a good time. I have other plans." A voice in his head told him to be more specific. "I'm really tied up all day today. I start my new job tomorrow and have so much to do."

"Oh, come on now. Looks to me like you have absolutely nothing going on. How about a drink, Jase?"

Feeling cornered and cowardly, Jason went to the refrigerator and grabbed two bottles of beer. Maybe if he gave in just a bit he could get rid of her quicker.

Annalise sat on the edge of the sofa, seduction bulging from her eyes. He handed her a bottle, taking a seat in the overstuffed chair across from her. An angry frown surfaced as daggers shot from her eyes, headed right for him. He could almost feel the hit. He chugged half his beer, paused and belched. Then he proceeded to slam down the second half.

Unamused, Annalise could feel her temper building. He was doing this on purpose and she knew it. The next belch, even louder, enraged her. Slamming her beer bottle down on the coffee table, she stood and put her hands on her hips, ready to fire.

"Jason Walker, you are truly the biggest asshole that ever lived."

She stormed to the dining room to snatch up her purse and stomped out the front door. Her fury hanging in the air like a cloud of dust, she slammed the front door shut, causing the knocker to rattle. Thankful to get Annalise out the door, Jason picked up his cell phone from the coffee table and dialed Lexi. He could hear her phone ringing from a distance, realizing she did not have it with her.

"Shit!"

He took off out the back door and headed straight for Mirror Pond. Her place of peace and comfort. When he arrived, she was nowhere to be found.

"She has to be here," he whispered.

Lexi and the pups headed straight for a nearby park that overlooked the Deschutes River. At the sight of the ducks, Sadie and Stout tugged on their leashes but Lexi resisted, directing them toward a small amphitheater that sat in the middle of the park. After finding a large ponderosa pine to cop a squat under, Lexi looked on as Sadie and Stout stuck their noses into the grass, tracking anything and everything. She pulled the bandanna from around her head and rubbed away the strain she felt with the palms of her hands. Tears began to pool and Lexi did not have the strength to fight them. She allowed the release, feeling the stream of water down her cheeks. Gazing at the amphitheater brought back memories of the multitude of times she, Christopher and Jason had come to the park to watch music and drama performances put on by the locals. Mrs. Taylor would send them off with a backpack full of snacks and sodas. She thought of one particular night when Christopher stayed behind because he had the stomach flu. Lexi had just turned sixteen. Her body was changing, her feminine side becoming more dominant each day.

* * *

"Lexi Jane, let's sit back here tonight," Jason had said, taking her hand to guide the way.

"But we can barely see anything this far back, Jason."

"Just, come on. Sit ... right here."

She looked at him quizzically as she surrendered to his demands. She pulled a red and black plaid blanket out of her backpack and threw it down on the grass. She bent down to smooth it out perfectly, and Jason sat next her, smiling mischievously. He looked around to make sure no one was looking before inconspicuously reaching behind his back to pull out a shiny silver flask. Lexi raised an eyebrow in question.

"What are you up to, Jason? What is that?"

He smiled and unscrewed the cap.

"Where did you get that?" she said as he took a large swallow.

He handed the flask over to her. "Go on, Lexi. Take a sip."

She took the flask from his grip, hesitant to partake.

"Haven't you ever snuck into your parents alcohol stash, Lexi?"

"No way, Jason. Momma and Daddy would have my hide."

She raised the flask to her lips, testing the waters. Jason stared and waited. The cold feel of steel hit her senses first, followed by the intense whiff of alcohol. She could taste it before the amber liquid hit her tongue. Jason lifted his hand to tip the flask back and keep her from stalling any longer.

"Whoa ... *cuh, cuh.* This is strong."

She could feel the warmth of the bourbon go through her bloodstream. Intrigued, she took another swig and wiped the dregs from her lips.

Jason took back the flask, indulging in more himself.

"I feel really good right now," Lexi said, laying her head in Jason's lap. "Can I have more?"

Jason hesitated. If he took Lexi home drunk, the Taylor's would be mad and disappointed. He didn't care for what that would feel like.

"Easy there. Too much of a good thing is not good. I can't take you home all silly and staggering."

She stared at him with the eyes of a vulnerable deer. Her hand came up to wrap around his leg. The other lightly stroked the front of his shirt. He swallowed the lump in his throat as he looked down at her inviting lips. Things were changing between them. It had been hard not to notice the angles and curves she'd developed. He could see a beautiful, mature young woman, not the sisterly brat he grew up with. The intimate feel of her hands and the look of desire in her eyes were seducing him. He ran his fingers through her vixenish hair. The erotic waves and tendrils felt like satin. He'd always wanted to touch the wild mane. When she was mad, the locks puffed out, looking coarse and sassy. The feel of it made him smile, warming his heart in a tender way.

Lexi watched, the look of admiration pleasing her. She wondered what he was thinking, hoping they were on the same intimate page.

The bourbon settling in her system encouraged a daring move. She lifted herself up to look into his eyes, leaning in closer to place a kiss on his lips. He accepted, wanting more. She licked her lips and waited. He kissed her again, feeling her arms wrap around his neck. Her soft lips and moist tongue sent his senses spiraling. All he could think about was laying her down on the blanket, kissing her endlessly and ravishing her body. But his mind began firing off, telling him to stop. The throbbing sensation in his pants begged for more. He pulled back, breaking their embrace, tossing the devil off his shoulder.

"Lexi ... I, um ... I think we should head back."

Jason got on his knees and began gathering their belongings and stuffing them into the pack. She stared, perplexed and heartbroken.

Jason stood, reaching out for her hand. "Come on. Let's go."

She ignored the gesture, picked up the blanket and began folding it, hoping to hide the tears that fell. An awkward silence hung in the air as they walked home. When they reached the rustic cabin, Jason grabbed her shoulders and looked directly at her. His heart leaped at the pain in her expression.

"I'm sorry, Lexi. I shouldn't have let this happen. We shouldn't do this, you know? The bourbon was a bad idea. This is my fault."

Lexi felt embarrassed and disappointed, so much emotion ready to regurgitate out of her body.

"Are you okay? Do you feel all right?" Jason said, hoping she hadn't drunk too much. He knew her system wasn't used to alcohol.

Her response was a bit chilly. "I am fine."

He knew what it really meant when a woman says she is fine.

* * *

Jason walked across the dock and gazed at the glassy water. The sun was beginning to go down and a slight breeze created ripples on the pond. He sat on the dock, laid his back down and closed his eyes. His thoughts took over. Lexi was one of the most important people in his life and he knew he was messing everything up. Just then, the sound of a large splash came from the pond, causing him to lunge forward. Sadie and Stout were swimming toward him. Lexi was on the other side, hands on her hips, staring at him. She looked around to see if Annalise was there. To her relief, she was nowhere to be found. Had Jason sent her away and come to the pond to find her?

Unsure what to do, Jason stood quietly to allow Lexi the first move. The receiving end of her anger was not the place to be. He watched intently as she began to take off her clothes.

What is happening?

Lexi eased into the pond until her entire body was submerged. He decided to follow suit, quickly peeling off his clothes. He dived in and met her halfway across. No words were spoken. Lexi wrapped her arms around his neck and literally began making love to his mouth. He responded without hesitation. She wrapped her legs around his waist as the buoyancy of the water carried them both. Pellets of water dripped into their mouths as they kissed, enhancing the moisture. Her breasts were pressed tightly against his chest and she rubbed her pelvis against his. It felt so good and she wanted more. She broke the kiss to speak. Jason's breathing heavy as he listened. She was hesitant, concerned about sharing her deepest secret with him.

"Jason, I have never made love before."

His eyes flew open in surprise. Their eyes were locked as he tried to process what she'd said. They floated in silence for what seemed like a lifetime. The look on her face exuded fear and vulnerability.

"Jason, please say something."

"Sorry. I'm caught off guard a bit. Shocked, actually. I know that I shouldn't be. You are still so young. We came very close to ... more than once. God, Lexi."

Lexi began to shiver, her lips quivering.

"You're cold. Let's get you out of this water and back home. Come on."

Jason grabbed her hand and they swam to the dock. After retrieving their clothes, they walked back to the house in silence.

"You should go take a hot shower, Lexi."

She stood directly in front of him, taking his hand. "Join me."

Jason swallowed. *Oh, God.*

He wanted to so very badly. But this was Lexi. How could he, knowing he would be taking her innocence? He could see Mr. and Mrs. Taylor in his mind. The guilt made him sick to his stomach.

Lexi could see the turmoil in his face and dropped his hand. "Forget it, Jason. We keep coming right back here. So close and then ... you shut it down. I can't do this anymore."

"Lexi—"

"It was terrifying for me to tell you that I am ... that I have never, you know? I was hoping you wouldn't freak out and run scared. It isn't like I haven't had opportunities to have sex. I haven't been with anyone I wanted to. I think I have always known that I wanted it to happen with you, Jason."

He stared at her, his heart wrenching. "Lexi. I—"

"I have just divulged to you the most intimate, private feelings I carry inside me. I don't want to hear the same old excuse about Chris being like a brother to you and blah, blah, blah. We are not the same people anymore. We are older and capable of making our own decisions. I wish you would stop being such a coward. If you want to be with me, then be with me. I don't get what is so hard about that. Christopher will understand. If he doesn't, then screw him."

She turned on her heels and in a few long strides made it to her bedroom without falling apart. She stood against her door, fighting the urge to kick it with her heel. She knew what she had to do. Giving up on Jason wouldn't happen overnight, but she had to find a way to let it go. The hope, the desire and the fantasy of ever truly belonging to him. No more disappointment and heartache. Let it go. That is what she would do.

CHAPTER SIX

Recruiting Lexi

"Alexis, I have got two fluff balls in the waiting room ready for you," Olivia said, filing charts near the front desk.

"Those would be chinchillas, Olivia." Lexi laughed, shaking her head.

"You know, I think you could get the Internet with all the pens stuck in your hair right now. Do you have a problem with pencil holders, Olivia?"

Olivia cocked her head and sneered. "Pa-lease go get those things and take them back. Those beady-eyed rodents are giving me the creeps."

"How is it you even got this job?" Lexi teased.

It had been one of those crazy days at the vet clinic. Everything from dogs to reptiles to furry rodents had been brought in. Dr. Stephenson and Lexi wished for roller skates to keep up. Olivia walked into the exam room, gasping at the sight of Lexi's last patient of the day.

"Oh my God. How can you even hold that thing? Are you mad?" Olivia backed up against the wall as she looked at the snake coiled around Lexi's hand.

Lexi stretched her hand out closer to her. Teasing and taunting, preying on Olivia's fears.

"Don't you dare get near me with that ... that slithering, venomous, rat-eating varmint."

"Venomous? Really? Good Lord. I think you need to go home, Olivia."

"I came back here to tell you that Colonel Bowman is here to see you."

"Oh, no. Is his K-9 Gunner sick?"

Olivia remained glued to the wall, stepping side to side, easing her way out of the examination room. "Nope. Just said he needed to talk you. I am leaving for the day. Friday can't get here soon enough. See you tomorrow."

Lexi put the snake away and walked her clients out the door.

"Colonel Bowman. What a pleasure to see you. Is everything okay with Gunner?"

The colonel stood to greet Lexi. He was tall, with a tight military haircut, his temples exposing gray hair. "Everything is fine with Gunner. Thank you. You have been on my mind, Alexis. Please, sit down. I hope you have a few minutes."

"For you, always, Colonel. What's up?"

"Alexis, have you ever considered the military?"

"What? Well, no. Never. I have always wanted to work with animals."

"Yes, of course. That is why I am here. Alexis, you would be an amazing K-9 handler. I feel strongly that you are the perfect candidate. There would be mandatory physical training, weapons training ... you get the picture. But I do not see that as an issue for you."

"You're here to recruit me?"

"I am simply putting an idea in your head and seeing where it takes you, Alexis. Please, think about it. Call me anytime to discuss things." He stood and shook Lexi's hand. "We could use more people like you, Alexis. Have a good night."

"Thank you, Colonel Bowman."

He walked out of the animal hospital, leaving Lexi stunned.

K-9 handler?

Her mind was processing. Would she even consider this? She cleaned and closed down the clinic for the night, running all the possibilities through her mind. It was a huge compliment that the colonel would consider her for this position. She couldn't help but think about how good it might be for her to leave town for a while ... and be away from Jason. Start over and try to move on. She needed to find a way to cleanse Jason from her system or she would never be able to give any other man a real chance. Jason had been all she ever wanted. It didn't seem that he would ever come around, and life was too short.

She grabbed her purse, turned out the lights and locked up for the night. Little did she know what would transpire sooner than later.

"Jason, do you have a second before you take off?" Gage asked.

"Uh, sure. Just wrapping things up here. Come on in."

Gage entered Jason's office, adjusted his blue tie and sat down. "So, how did your first day go?"

"A little overwhelming, but that was to be expected. I have plenty of projects to keep myself busy for a long time." He leaned back in his office chair. "I'm dying to ask, Gage. How did things go with Annalise Saturday night? I am sure she stuck to you like sweet honey."

"Yes. Thanks a lot for that. The thing is, she talked about you most of the night. Since you brought it up, I'm actually a lot more interested in getting to know Alexis. Is she seeing anyone?"

Gage interested in Lexi? Over my dead body. "I really don't know. I haven't been home from Seattle that long. Haven't had a chance to really catch up with everyone."

"Mm-hmm ... Well, do you think you could set something up for the two of us? An impromptu meeting of sorts?"

Jason did not like this one bit. No way, no how. "Let me feel things out first. You can understand that, right? I have known Lexi my whole life."

Gage stood up to pat Jason on the back. "Gotcha. The big brother thing. I get it."

Jason stood. "No, no. Not a big brother thing."

"I will catch you tomorrow. See ya, Jason."

Jason scratched the back of his head. His boss wanted to date Lexi. The reality was, if not Gage, it would inevitably be some other man. Lexi wouldn't stay single forever and she sure as hell had written him off. Maybe it would be for the best if they both started dating other people. It would make things less complicated.

Who was he kidding? The thought of another man touching Lexi made him insane with jealousy. It was a "damned if I do, damned if I don't" situation. He lacked the nerve to address Christopher honestly about the possibilities. He tapped his pen nervously on the table. Maybe he was underestimating his best friend.

The vibration of his cell phone diverted his attention. "Oh, shit. Annalise."

His eyes shot open wide after reading her text: "I am heading over to your house. See you soon."

Crap. She was determined not to give up. Jason looked at his watch and realized Lexi would most likely be home.

"Great."

He bolted out of his office and headed home in his truck like a bat out of hell.

Annalise sat on the couch with her legs crossed and her arms folded over her chest. Lexi had let her in but had no intention of entertaining her.

She kept herself busy in the kitchen and could hear Annalise sigh with impatience as she waited for Jason.

"Lexi, can you do something with your dogs, please? They are staring at me like I'm an intruder."

Lexi poked her head into the living room, smiling mischievously. The dogs were getting a treat tonight.

"Don't you know anything about dogs, Annalise? They are very intuitive animals. They are looking at you like that for a reason. Sadie, Stout ... come here." She bent down when they greeted her and pet them vigorously as if to say "good boy, good girl." Just then, she heard the front door creak open.

"Uh, Jason," Annalise said. "Finally. I didn't think you would ever get here." Her brow furrowed, she looked in Lexi's direction.

Jason smiled, knowing exactly what Annalise was referring to. The tension in the air was nearly suffocating. She stood up from the couch and began her sultry approach, but Sadie and Stout beat her to it. They were all over Jason, tails wagging and tongues licking.

"Okay, okay, you guys. I'm happy to see you, too. Let's get down now. Hey, Annalise. What brings you by ... again?"

In the background, Jason could hear Lexi banging things around in the kitchen. His eyes wandered in that direction, but Annalise grabbed his chin, redirecting his attention.

"Jason, eyes on me. I thought we could, you know, spend some time together, baby."

Lexi rolled her eyes in disgust. Annalise was a piece of work. She clearly hadn't gotten the hint yesterday. That Jason could be genuinely interested in her was mind-boggling. If sex was all you cared about, Annalise was your girl.

"Tonight is not good, Annalise," Jason said. "I am wiped out. I appreciate you stopping by."

The back of her hand brushed his cheek. "Don't make me wait too long, Jason. Call me," she whispered into his ear.

Her hips swayed as she made her way to the front door. She looked at Jason and winked before shutting the door behind her.

Jason took a deep breath, preparing himself before heading to the kitchen.

"Hey, Lexi. Sorry about that. I didn't invite her here."

All he could see was her backside. He stood patiently with his hands on his hips, waiting for her to turn around. He rubbed his chin, feeling the bristles that had already begun to form since shaving just that morning. He moved a little closer to Lexi. She looked over her shoulder and decided to desist. She turned around to face him, arms behind her back against the countertop. She had changed out of her blue scrubs into a black sweatshirt that hung off one shoulder and gray cotton shorts that fit like a glove.

"This is your house, too, Jason. It is not for me to say who you have over here. Anyway, how was your first day? Gage seems like he will be great to work with."

The hair on the back of Jason's neck stood up. Now Lexi was mentioning Gage? What was going on here?

"Time will tell, I suppose. I have a lot of work ahead of me."

Sadie and Stout raced to the front door as it slammed shut. Christopher stomped his feet on the mat, wiping the bottom of each boot with vigor.

"Lexi Jane!" he yelled, his voice carrying throughout the house.

She looked at Jason in confusion and headed for the living room.

"Christopher? What are you doing home? I thought you were gone until Friday."

"Never mind that. I just ran into Colonel Bowman in the driveway. He said to give you this packet. What the hell is going on, Lexi?"

"Just calm down, Chris. Let me take a look."

Jason was right on her heels, wondering what the drama was about.

She opened the big manila envelope and pulled out several pages. Jason and Christopher crowded in close, looking over her shoulder.

"Guys, could you give me a little room here?" she said.

Flipping through the pages, she blew out a long breath and paused to reflect.

"Well? What is this all about, Lexi?" Christopher said.

Jason and Christopher stared at her, brows furrowed, waiting for an answer.

She cleared her throat, wondering why she felt so nervous. "Well, it is actually pretty amazing news. Colonel Bowman came by the clinic today to see if I might be interested in K-9 training. Military K-9 training. He feels I would be the perfect candidate."

"What? No. No." Christopher said, shaking his head.

"Excuse me? This is not your decision, Christopher."

"You can't go into the military," Jason said. "I mean, what about Sadie and Stout? Are you just going to leave them behind?"

"I have thought about Sadie and Stout, and, yes, it is a concern for me. Is that all that bothers you, Jason?"

"The thing is, Lexi," Christopher said, "even if you enlist and get through boot camp, there is no guarantee that you will get that particular specialty. You could get stuck working at a desk somewhere and you would hate it. If you do get picked for K-9 handling, you will be sent to the most dangerous places. Have you even thought about all the possibilities?" He was staring down at her, hands on his hips.

"I haven't had the chance to do any thinking at all. This just came up."

"Are you actually considering this?" Jason said.

"Why shouldn't I consider it? It is an honor to be asked, and what exactly is keeping me *here*, Jason Walker?"

He reeled back in shock. She had him by the balls.

"Maybe we should all calm down," Christopher said. "Lexi is right. This is her decision to make. I don't like it, but it is her choice one way or another. Please, just take your time. Make sure you know exactly what you are getting yourself into."

Lexi shoved the papers back into the manila envelope. "You have to stop treating me like a child. I would never jump into anything this important without proper thought and research." She dropped the packet onto the kitchen table and walked to the back door, noticing the clouds rolling in. "There is supposed to be a storm moving in tonight. I am going to take Sadie and Stout out before it hits. I will do my own thing for dinner."

Thunder cracked like a sonic boom, making Lexi's room so bright it blinded her eyes for a quick minute. Ever since that day fishing at Mirror Pond years ago, storms made her feel restless. Sadie and Stout were curled up as close as they could get to her. Poor Sadie shivered in fear.

"It's okay, girl. Come on."

The covers flew off the bed as the threesome quietly sneaked into Jason's room. This wasn't the first time that his room had been a safe haven for her and the pups when a storm was roaring angrily.

Dragging her blanket with her, they made their way to the corner of the room, where she found comfort in an oversize chair and ottoman. Sadie and Stout lay down below her feet. Feeling instant relief, Lexi fell asleep in seconds.

An hour or so later, Jason woke up to the sound of snoring. He sat up quickly to find the crew in the corner of his room. Stout was going to town with quite a rumble. Jason's mouth curled in an endearing smile. It had been a long time since he had seen this picture, and it got to him.

He climbed out of bed and hovered over Lexi, watching her sleep. Crouching to get a bit closer, he swept the hair away from her forehead and kissed her. Then his lips traveled from her forehead to her mouth. He could feel her breath against his face. He left a gentle kiss on her lips. Lexi stirred and her eyes fluttered open.

"Jason?" she whispered.

He didn't say a word as he looked into her questioning eyes. Her hands came up to cradle his face as she planted her lips firmly on his. One kiss after another with urgency. Jason pulled back to pick Lexi up from the overstuffed chair and carried her to his bed. Sadie's and Stout's heads popped up as they watched, but they didn't dare move.

Jason laid Lexi down and crawled into the bed next to her, pulling the covers over them. He maneuvered himself on top of her and she opened her legs to accommodate his presence. They kissed each other, releasing all the desire that had been locked up for so long. They tasted, stroked and touched each other. Lexi could feel his erection pressing against her. He moaned with desire, and she couldn't help but wonder if he would stop midstream with regret.

"Jason, I want to make love to you. It has to be you. No one else."

Jason knew that was what he needed, too. It was selfish, but for the first time, he didn't have any thoughts of backing out. Fuck Christopher.

"I want you, too, Lexi."

She smiled with relief and the excitement built. He lifted her shirt and slid his hand underneath. She could feel the palm of his hand, followed by the gentle touch of his fingertips around her nipple. His lips never left her mouth as he rolled her nipple between his fingertips, causing it to go erect. He pulled Lexi's shirt over her head and tossed it aside. He bent his head down to suck on her breast, and she could feel a tingling sensation in her vulva. She shivered at his touch.

Her fingers raked through his hair, ultimately coercing his head closer to her breast. Jason squeezed her breast to take more into his mouth.

More tingling. She could barely speak through the deep breaths of desire.

His mouth released her breast and found its way to the corner of her neck. As he left gentle kisses up and down the side of it, his hand explored down her torso, stopping at the waistband of her shorts. His fingers lifted the cotton fabric, being sure to dig deep enough past her panties. He located the softness of her tuft, processing the texture. The feel was slightly coarse. There wasn't a tundra of hair, only the perfect landscape. So female. Her hips moved in anticipation of his next move.

She felt his fingers dive into the depths of her desire, sending her spiraling.

There were no words spoken, yet the communication was abundant. Jason removed the rest of her clothing, followed by his own. He paused to look at her. *God, she is beautiful.* Looking into her eyes, he searched for any sign of fear or second thoughts. There were none.

"A lot of pressure, Lexi. Let me know if you need me to stop."

She nodded and pulled him close. The sensation of his penis entering her caused her back to arch and her legs to tighten against him.

"Try to relax, baby. It will get easier."

She did as he said, and before she knew it, her body stopped resisting the pain, allowing him access with ease. Pain turned to pleasure.

She could feel his momentum begin to increase, his breathing become more labored by the second. She kept up with the pace, yearning for it to never end. She longed to share the most intimate part of herself with Jason. There would never be enough.

RECRUITING LEXI | 59

One last thrust and he groaned with ecstasy. He settled himself closely next to her.

"Are you okay, Lexi?" he said, brushing the hair from her flushed cheeks.

She smiled, nodding.

He pulled her close and kissed the top of her head. He noticed movement from the corner of his eye.

"Lexi. Stout is beside the bed staring at me with disapproving eyes. Don't judge me, Stout. Back to the corner. Go on!" He urged the protective pup to mind with a swift movement of his index finger. "Most men have dads to worry about. I have Stout."

Lexi pulled the sheets to cover her face, hiding the laughter and amusement. Dogs were the least of Jason's concern. Sooner or later, he would have to face Christopher.

He pulled Lexi in, encouraging her to be the small spoon. The storm continued to roar with fury. His arms enclosed her more securely. Every thunder strike awakened the demons from the past. He would never forget leaving Lexi all alone at the pond all those years ago.

* * *

Lexi pulled with all the force she had to reel the bugger in.

"Come on, I got you," she said, ignoring the weather disturbance.

The mighty force of the wind created a resistance, making it even harder to get the job done. Thunder growled so deeply that she could feel vibration. She closed her eyes in anticipation of what was sure to come next, never letting go of the pole. The sky lit up brightly.

Crack ... boom!

The strike hit close, causing the dock to shake like an earthquake. Lexi lost her footing, screaming as she went down.

Don't let go of the pole, Lexi. Do not let go.

One hand shot out to brace her fall and the other held on tight to the fishing pole. But not tight enough. The fish fought to get away, tugging hard, and the pole flew out of her hand.

"Oh, no. No, no, no!"

There was only one thing to do: dive in after it. She got up and jumped into the pond, hoping the fish was still on the line. Her head bobbed up out of the water and she wiped the water from her eyes. All she could see were bright orange flames. The strike had started a fire.

"Huh? ... Oh my God."

She swam in a circle to check her surroundings, hearing a voice in the distance.

"Lexi! Lexi!" Jason yelled.

He pushed past tree branches, running as fast as he could to get to her. At last he had a clear path to the pond, but he stopped short, staring in shock at the burning flames. His eyes roamed in every direction searching for Lexi.

"Lex-eeee!" he called. Again and again.

He could hear the faint sounds of emergency vehicles. He got closer to the dock, and there she was dragging herself out of the pond. Meanwhile, Mother Nature knew she had a job to do. The rain picked up, slowly smoldering the fire. Jason closed the distance between them. Lexi was completely soaked, smiling from ear to ear.

"I got it, Jason. Take a look at this beauty," Lexi said, holding a rainbow trout right up to his face.

His breathing, labored from fear and running, caused him to bend over. Holding on to his knees, he looked up at her. "You are crazy, Lexi Jane Taylor."

Grabbing her hand, he guided their way back to the house, where Mrs. Taylor waited anxiously on the back deck, watching for them. Lexi waved her arm to catch her attention. She stopped walking to proudly hold up her score.

"Momma! Momma, fish for dinner tonight."

CHAPTER SEVEN

Love and Destruction

Lexi stirred as her body clock told her it was time to wake up and get ready for work. As her eyes fluttered open, she realized where she was.

"Holy shit, Jason. I have to get out of your room before Chris wakes up."

She threw the covers back, bolted out of bed and carefully opened his bedroom door. Peeking her head out, she determined that the coast was clear. Sadie and Stout took off down the hall toward the back patio door. Lexi followed to let them out.

"Good morning."

Lexi jumped in surprise, turning around to find her brother sitting in the living room. She could only see the top of his head as he tied his shoes.

"You're up? Already?" she said nervously.

"Yeah. Just like every work morning. You seem to have slept in."

Oh, no. Did he know? Her body shifted nervously.

"No. Of course not. I am up … ready to go."

Christopher rested his hands on his knees and stared at Lexi, squinting his eyes in suspicion.

"God, I need coffee," she said and headed for the kitchen as a diversion. She fumbled around to make coffee, knocking things over and nearly dropping a glass. Christopher stood at the counter watching the comical event.

"What is with you today, Lexi? Maybe coffee isn't such a good idea for you this morning."

Lexi turned around and completely caved. "Okay, okay. I slept with Jason."

Christopher's eyes shot wide open. "*You did what*?"

He turned on his heels, heading for Jason's bedroom.

"Christopher, stop! Stop right now!" she yelled, chasing after him.

He grabbed the door knob and pushed it open with force. The first thing to catch his attention was that Jason's bed was in disarray. He threw his hands up to the side of his head.

"Oh my God. Oh … *my God!*"

Lexi reached out to touch Christopher's arm. "Chris, this is not a bad thing. Can we please talk about it?"

Right then, Jason strolled out of the bathroom, white towel around his waist and water dripping from the tips of his curls. Lexi couldn't help but notice the water droplets dangling from the hairs on his chest.

"Lexi, go put some clothes on right now!" Christopher said.

"I do have clothes on."

"Well, you need to put more on. Cover up, Lexi."

Jason looked back and forth from one sibling to the other. "Oh shit. You told him, Lexi?"

Lexi held up her index finger, gesturing for Jason to wait. "Just one second, Jason. Christopher, I am not a child or yours to order around. I will wear what I want and sleep with who I want."

Jason ran his hand over his face, perplexed by the conversation.

"This is between Jason and I. It doesn't involve you, Christopher."

"Jason, how could you?" Christopher said. "How long has this been going on?" Hands on his hips, he fought the urge to left hook his best friend.

Lexi walked over to stand next to Jason, ready to back him up.

"It just happened, Chris. This is the first time."

Lexi's head snapped to look at Jason in shock. "Wait, what? This has been something we have been building up to for years and not the first time we have fooled around, Jason Walker. You are making it sound like it was something we did on a whim."

"Lexi—"

"You are hiding things from me and apparently stringing my sister along, Jason," Christopher said. "I need to get out of here. This is so fucked up." He stormed out of the bedroom.

Tears pooled in Lexi's eyes. "I can't believe you didn't stand up for us, Jason."

"This is incredibly complicated, Lexi. I have been trying to tell you this. Then, straight away you run and tell him. We didn't even have a chance to discuss *what* we were going to do next."

Her arms were folded across her chest as she reached up to swipe away the tears running down her cheeks. "I didn't mean to. I felt so nervous and guilty. It just spewed out."

Sadie and Stout circled Lexi, looking up at her with worried eyes. Her hand came down to pet them. They were the most loyal and loving beings in her life. "Last night was the happiest of my life and it is all ruined."

"Lexi, don't say that."

"Well, you haven't done a single thing to reassure me. Chris is mad, yes, but I still want a chance at a relationship with you, Jason."

Jason sat in the overstuffed chair in the corner and covered his face with his hands. He blew out a long breath in frustration. "Lexi, we need to calm the storm. That is all I can think about right now. I'm sorry."

The pain in her heart felt like a deep internal burn. Everything looked blurry. She squeezed her eyes together tight to refocus. At a loss for words, she walked out of his room, gently shutting the door behind her.

She realized that she would be late for work and sprinted to her bedroom to retrieve her cell phone.

"Hey, Olivia. Everything is fine. Just running late. See you soon."

She dropped the phone onto her bed. From the corner of her eye, she spotted the large manila envelope from Colonel Bowman sitting on top of her dresser. She picked it up and held it against her chest. Her intuition warned her.

Make the right decision for you. Not because you are running.

Several days had gone by. No one in the Taylor house was speaking to each other, and enough was enough. Jason decided to make the first attempt at peace. He spotted Christopher out back chopping firewood. He walked down the stairs, gearing up for battle.

"Need a hand?" he asked, picking up a log and putting it on the stack.

Christopher paused, swiping the sweat from his forehead. He returned to chopping, now more vigorously.

"It's about time we talk, don't you think?" Jason said.

Christopher laughed in midswing. "Talking would have been a good idea a long time ago." He put the ax down on the ground and rested his forearm on it.

"Why didn't you say anything to me about what was happening with you and Lexi?"

"I have been fighting it. I feared it would upset you and ruin our friendship. My feelings for Lexi sparked months before I left for college. Going away to school had been the perfect diversion. I came home hoping the feelings wouldn't still be there. But obviously they are. She is hurt and furious.

I don't blame her. So here I am—the two most important people in my life hate me right now."

Christopher shook his head. "You really did fuck things up. Did it ever cross your mind that I might be happy about you and Lexi?"

"Not once. Guess I was right."

"Only because I didn't see this coming. It made my bloody head spin."

Jason couldn't help but smirk.

Christopher tossed the ax aside, getting right into Jason's face. "Look. I will be fine. You need to make things right with Lexi. You should have supported her. Figure out what you want and be honest with her."

Jason nodded. "Okay. I will handle this. I will make it right."

He felt ashamed for the way he'd handled the situation with Lexi. He turned to go back into the house, hoping she would be home from work. She had been coming home later than usual, no doubt avoiding him. He pulled out his cell phone to call her. No luck.

He decided to freshen up and go looking for her. When he stepped into his closet, a horrific smell stopped him in his tracks.

"Oh, God. What is that stench?"

Covering his nose, he did some detective work to find where the odor was coming from. He bent down to dig around his laundry basket on the floor.

"Shit! That damn cat peed on my clothes."

He picked up the basket and headed for the basement to throw his clothes in the washer. He grabbed a clothespin and quickly put it on his nose.

"Oh, this is nasty. I bet Lexi would just love this."

"Love what?" Lexi asked, looking down at him from the top of the stairs.

Jason turned around to face her, clothespin still attached. She slowly walked down the steps as she waited for his answer.

"Patches decided to pee in my laundry basket. My clothes are probably ruined, Lexi Jane."

She was mad as hell at Jason, but in that moment she could not help laughing. His voice sounded nasally and his eyes watered. Giggling, she covered her mouth with her hand.

"Laugh it up, Lexi."

"I told you cats were intuitive."

He removed the clothespin and leaned against the washer. They stared at each other in silence. Lexi turned to head back up the steps.

"Lexi, wait. We need to talk."

Ignoring his words, she continued up the steps.

"Lexi! You are such a stubborn sass. Come back here."

She was in the process of removing her blue scrubs when Jason burst through her bedroom door without knocking. She quickly covered her chest.

"Jason! Get out of here."

Refusing to leave, he turned around to respect her privacy. "I'm not going anywhere until we talk."

She pulled out a black satin robe from the closet to cover herself.

Jason turned around, finding himself speechless. His temper softened as he admired her. The satin garment shimmered in the light. She had taken her hair down from a bun, exposing a wild mane.

Lexi looked at Jason with fury in her eyes. They glowed like raging flames. He took a few steps toward her. Her expression didn't falter as he got closer. Much closer. He put his hands on top of her shoulders.

"Lexi," he whispered.

She placed her hands on his chest, pushing him back. "No, Jason. No."

"I am so sorry, Lexi."

"You initiated the kiss, Jason. You said that you wanted me, too. You betrayed me."

"Yes. I didn't mean to. Everything happened so fast."

"We need some distance, Jason. I have to ... not want you." Tears surfaced, revealing her vulnerability.

"No. Lexi, can't we please start over? Move forward from this? I don't regret our night together."

She grabbed a tissue from the box on her dresser to soak up the remnants from the dam that had broken. Her heart and her head were on two different channels. "Well, I do."

"Lexi, don't say that."

She pushed him away again. "I regret it, Jason! Get out of my room and leave me alone."

Jason felt nauseated and his heart ached. His gut told him he'd lost Lexi forever. He wanted desperately to protest and keep trying. Instead, he walked out of her bedroom, fully aware that the door would be closed indefinitely.

CHAPTER EIGHT

The Rebound

Olivia typed away at her computer, becoming distracted by the ringing bell of the front office door. Her eyes opened wide as a handsome gentleman approached the counter. He wore a crisp-looking dark gray suit with a bright blue tie. He flashed a dazzling white smile, charming her like a cobra.

"Good afternoon. My name is Gage. I stopped by to say hello to Alexis. Is it possible to have a few minutes of her time?"

"Are you a drug rep or ..."

"No, no. This would be a personal visit." He noticed the selection of pencils in her hair. He pointed to the French twist supporting the supply.

"You, um, seem to have misplaced a few writing utensils."

Olivia threw her hands up to her head, smiling bashfully. "You can never have enough. Every time I turn around, I can't find anything to write with."

"No kidding. So ... Alexis?"

Olivia jumped nervously from her computer chair. "Right. Let me go see if she is available. Last time I saw her she had a thermometer up a dog's ... You don't really need to know that. Okay, be right back. Have a seat. Make yourself comfortable."

Gage privately rolled his eyes. The poor lady was rambling. "Thank you."

Olivia searched the back office for Alexis. "Where is she? Alexis? Alexis!"

"What, Olivia? I am in the lab running blood work."

"Put that down. Right now. There is an incredibly gorgeous man in the waiting room asking for you. Gage. Delicious."

"Gage? Really? Okay, give me five. I will come out."

"Who is he?"

"He is Jason's boss. I met him a few weeks ago. I wonder why he is here to see me."

Olivia stared at Lexi expectantly.

"Olivia? Could you please go let him know I will be right with him?"

"Yes, of course. Hurry up, though."

Olivia turned on her heels to deliver the message. She found Gage standing by the front window, hands in his pockets waiting patiently.

"Alexis, will be right with you."

Gage waved in response, afraid to return to the front desk.

Lexi delivered the blood results to Dr. Stephenson, quietly leaving him to interpret them. "I will be right back, Doc."

She used her hands to smooth her uniform and fluff away accumulated animal hair. Lifting the collar of her shirt, she took a whiff to see if she smelled like dog. Feeling presentable enough, she entered the waiting room. Gage smiled as soon as they made eye contact.

"Hi Gage. Good to see you again. What brings you by today?"

Lexi held out her hand to initiate a handshake. From the corner of her eye, she could detect that Olivia was spying intently from behind the counter.

"Hello, Alexis. I wanted to come by and see if you would be interested in meeting up with me for a drink or dinner?" Gage's eyes shifted to Olivia and his brow furrowed. "Does she do that often? Curious woman."

Lexi laughed as she spun her head around, squinting her eyes to signal Olivia to knock it off. Olivia smiled bashfully and directed her attention to busy work.

"Don't mind her. Small town. You have obviously made an impression."

"Well, I hope you feel the same way. What do you say? Drink?"

The warning bells rang loudly in her mind, nearly causing her to touch her forehead. She wanted to say yes.

Why shouldn't I say yes?

"I would love to. I have some errands after work, but how about we meet at the seafood restaurant at the Old Mill District around seven?"

Gage touched the side of her arm, squeezing slightly. "Great. I will see you then, Alexis."

She smiled as he released her arm and left the clinic. Her hands found their way inside her shirt pockets. She knew what was coming next.

"Don't say a word, Olivia."

"Oh, come on. He asked you out, didn't he?"

Lexi kept walking and slipping into an unoccupied examination room. She paced back and forth in the small space, talking to herself.

What am I doing? Is this a revenge date? Am I that girl? Oh, but he is good-looking and nice, too. I would be crazy not to see where this goes. But, Jason ... Oh, forget him.

Dr. Stephenson tapped on the door.

"Everything okay in there, Alexis?"

"Yep, just tidying up," she said.

He leaned his ear a bit closer to the door. He was sure he heard crazy chatter. For several days he'd felt something was not quite right.

"Let me know if you need anything."

Lexi smiled. Dr. Stephenson had a heart of gold. She always got a kick out of his belly bulge that left gaping holes around the buttons. His jolly personality and kind demeanor were loved by all.

"Thank you, Doctor. I am about done in here." She pulled her cell phone out of her back pocket. *It is time to call Colonel Bowman.*

Jason's pickup truck idled at the stoplight. He became lost in his thoughts about Lexi.

I bet a visit to the pond will soften her up. Give me a chance to talk this mess out.

A honking sound from behind his truck brought his attention back to the traffic signal.

"Oh, shit. Sorry," he said, waving apologetically to the SUV behind him.

He eased into the intersection, looking both ways to make sure it was clear. The sight of Lexi's black Jeep Wrangler caught his eye. There was only one in town like it. Oversize tires, lift kit and KC lights mounted on top. She was every man's dream girl. A chick who liked trucks, could shoot any type of gun with accuracy and loved fishing and camping. She could even keep up with most sports.

He slowed the truck down to pull into the parking lot. Trying to be discreet, he picked a space several rows back. Glancing up and down the businesses in the strip mall, he tried to figure out which one she was patronizing. One of the glass doors read *ARMY* in big bold letters.

Oh, no. She is going to run. She is going to enlist just to get away from me. This is not going to happen.

He jumped out of the truck, slammed the door shut and took off for the recruiting office. Walking in the door with determination, he scanned the room for Lexi.

"Excuse me, sir. May I help you?" an Army recruiter said.

"Uh, yes sir. I am here for Lexi. Alexis Jane Taylor. I do believe she is here."

"I am sorry. I cannot divulge personal information on the whereabouts of a new recruit."

Jason's mouth dropped open. "New recruit? I am too late. Oh my God. Lexi, no." His hand brushed over his face. "This is all my fault."

"I think it would be a good idea if you left the premises, sir."

"No. You don't understand. I need to see her right now. Lexi!" he yelled across the office, drawing everyone in the office to the front room. Lexi heard the commotion and followed suit.

"Jason? What is going on? What are you doing here?" she said, mortified.

Jason latched on to the top of her shoulders. "Lexi, don't do this. Is it too late to withdraw? Just, come home with me. I am not going to let you run."

"What? You think I am running? Screw you, Jason Walker. Not that it is any of your business, but I didn't enlist."

"You didn't? Oh, thank God. I don't know what you were thinking even considering it."

Lexi knocked his hand off her shoulder, breaking away from his clutches.

"Hey. Do you have to be so angry? What is with you, Lexi?"

"Leave me alone, Jason. You have already made me late for my date."

Lexi stormed out of the office. She sat in her Jeep, feeling it was quite possible she could spit blood. Her wrists twisted and turned around the steering wheel.

"That cocky son of a biscuit eater."

She looked down at her blue scrubs, realizing she had to go home and change before her date with Gage.

"Great. Just great."

Meanwhile, a dozen pairs of threatening eyes stared Jason down.

"I apologize for the disturbance," he said. "It is not what you think. Lexi and I grew up together. I was trying to save her from making a big mistake. Stubborn woman."

He left the office furious, recalling the conversation in his head.

Oh, she has a date. Well, good for her. I hope he enjoys the cyclone of attitude he will endure.

Lexi walked into the restaurant, checking her watch to see how late she was.

Not too bad. Just a few minutes.

She wore a navy blue halter top dress with four-inch tan wedge sandals. The breeze blew her hair as she walked to the back patio, exposing a hint of her dangling gold earrings.

There he is.

She waved and headed for the table overlooking the river. Gage stood to greet her.

"You are stunning," he said, bending down to kiss her cheek.

She knew the endearment should have felt nice, but instead she felt uncomfortable. So as not to be rude, she smiled and sat down.

"I am glad you agreed to this, Alexis. I tried weeks ago to get Jason to set something up between us. You know, a bit discreetly so we could get to know each other."

Lexi's face went flat. "Oh, really."

"Yeah. I get it. He was feeling protective in a big brother sort of way. I got tired of waiting and decided to ask you out myself."

Her foot tapped with irritation as she processed. "Huh. Isn't that nice. He is so concerned for my well-being." She gestured for the server to come to their table. "Drinks. We need drinks." If she didn't pull herself together, she would ruin the entire evening.

Gage put his hand on top of hers. "I was thinking we could order a bottle of champagne."

Champagne? A tall cold beer is what she had in mind. "Oh, sure. Nice. Thank you."

Gage smiled, ordering the bottle of bubbles and two chicken Caesar salads. And so the cyclone began.

"Hold on. I am perfectly capable of ordering for myself, Gage." She caught the server before he walked away. "Could you scratch that, please? I will have a ribeye steak, medium rare, with a loaded baked potato, and let's finish it off with roasted vegetables."

She turned to smile at Gage. There was a message projecting through the agitated curve of her lips and he read it loud and clear. Loosening his light blue tie, he felt nervous and started to sweat. He'd never had this reaction on a date before. Clearing his throat, he tried desperately to recover and move the date in a more positive direction.

"Tonight would be the perfect evening for a walk along the river after dinner."

Lexi decided to stand down and work on her people skills. "Sure. Sounds great."

"I can't help but feel you are agitated this evening, Alexis. Have I done something?"

"No. I'm sorry, Gage. I shouldn't have been so rude. To be honest with you, I had a spat with Jason before I came here." She shook her head. "He just makes me crazy sometimes. I'm sorry. This is so inappropriate. Not very good first date conversation is it?"

Gage stood, offering his hand to her. "Come on. Let's go take that walk."

She smiled as she took his hand. Their fingers linked, fitting like a puzzle. He led her to a bridge nearby, where they stopped to take in the scenery.

"I love it here," Lexi said.

"I am loving it more and more. Especially now."

Gage felt the moment to be romantic. He gently stroked her bare back as he bent down to kiss her. She closed her eyes, waiting for the feel of his lips. The kiss was soft, nice. Both his hands moved to her waist, pulling her closer. His mouth went for her lips again. Lexi played along until he slipped his tongue inside. Her arms came up like armor pushing him back. He wiped the moisture from his lips with the back of his hand.

"I'm sorry, Gage. Let's take things down a notch, all right?"

"All right. My apologies." His tone projected irritation, with a hint of sarcasm beneath it.

"Come on. Let's go have our dinner and try to get to know each other," she said, gesturing for them to start walking.

The evening remained awkward, marked by small talk.

"My dinner was great. Thank you very much, Gage."

"I wish the evening had gone better, Alexis. Let me walk you to your car."

Guilt, sadness and regret were taking her emotions on a wild ride. She'd really blown it tonight. She knew the demon responsible for interfering in what could have been an amazing night.

Gage watched as she pulled out of the parking lot. He waited a few seconds, got into his own car and began following her. He stayed back just far enough not to be spotted, following her all the way to her house. He discreetly parked in front of a neighbor's house down the street and turned off the engine. He looked around to make sure no one was watching. Chewing on his thumbnail, he watched Lexi go into the house, noting that Jason's pickup wasn't present. He removed his tie, threw it on the passenger seat and opened the top button of his shirt. His eyes turned dark as the pupils dilated. The living room lit up in the Taylor house. Next came Lexi's bedroom.

Sadie and Stout circled round and round Lexi, tails wagging like whips.

"I bet you guys need to go out. Come on. Let's go."

They flew out the back door. Lexi stood on the porch, keeping a close eye on her pups. The temperature had gone down significantly. She wrapped her arms around her shoulders in an effort to warm up. The sky was clear, Venus shining with dominance. She peeked back inside the house, noticing that the front door was wide open.

"What the heck? Sadie! Stout! Come on!" she whistled, encouraging them to come quickly.

Lexi let the dogs into the house, following cautiously. If someone was in the house, Sadie and Stout would find them. They headed straight for her bedroom. She shut the front door and locked it securely. When she reached her bedroom, Sadie and Stout were sniffing around the window. The curtains were fluttering. Someone had opened the window, but the screen was still attached. She did a quick scan of the room, running for the closet where she kept her Glock. After punching in the security numbers on the lock box, she retrieved her weapon and dialed Christopher.

"Chris. I need you to come home. Please hurry. Someone has been in our house."

Chapter Nine

Shady Happenings

Jason walked out of the downtown whiskey bar and paused to assess whether driving was a good idea. As he swayed one way and then the other, his question was answered. Fumbling to find his cell phone, he felt it in the front pocket of his jeans. He dialed Christopher as he leaned against the streetlight pole.

"Hey, man. I had one too many. Can you come pick me up?"

"Shit, Jason. Your timing sucks. I have a situation at home. The cops are here. I don't want to leave Lexi."

Jason kicked the back of his heel to break the brace the pole had on him. Concern flooded his veins, nearly sobering him in the process.

"What the hell is going on? Is Lexi okay?"

"She is fine. Just freaked out. Someone came into the house, brazen enough to do it while she was outside with the dogs. I will tell you all about it when you get home. Can you walk home or—"

"I will figure it out. I am on my way."

"Officer, I usually lock the front door when I come home. For some reason tonight ... well, I just didn't."

"And, you never opened the window in your bedroom?" the officer said.

"I definitely did not."

Jason came through the front door and walked quietly into the living room to listen in.

Lexi glanced his way, noting the look of concern in his eyes.

"So, nobody else who lives here was in your room and opened the window?" the officer said, looking over at Christopher and Jason.

"No, it wasn't me," Christopher said. "Jason?" He glared, lifting a quizzical brow at his friend.

"Don't look at me. I have been gone all day." His eyes scanned the room. He felt like he was in the middle of a full-on interrogation.

"Lexi, is there anyone who would be stalking you? An ex-boyfriend or someone you have been on a date with recently?"

Jason folded his arms, staring her down. She *had* been on a date. But with who?

"I went out with a gentleman this evening. I, um ... I met up with him at the restaurant. He has never been here, to my knowledge."

"Who were you out with?" Christopher said.

Lexi cleared her throat, looking back and forth between Jason and her brother.

"I had dinner with Gage."

Jason's eyes bulged with rage. "You have got to be kidding me. Gage? That is the date you were on?"

Christopher stepped in front of Jason. "Not now, Jason. Your jealous temper won't help."

Jason turned his back on the people in the room and stepped away.

The officer focused his attention back on Lexi, dismissing Jason's tantrum. "How did the date go, Lexi?"

"It was fine. Just your normal first date, I guess. A little new and awkward. There weren't any red flags to suggest that he would do something like this."

"Okay. I will report all of this. If you remember anything else or notice something unusual in the future, be sure to tell me, Lexi. Be aware of your surroundings."

Lexi stood, holding her hand out to shake the officer's hand. "Thank you very much, Officer Jenkins. I will let you know if anything comes up."

Christopher escorted the officer to his car, leaving Jason and Lexi alone to stew.

"You don't think Annalise would do something like this, do you, Jason?"

Turning back around to face her, he lifted his shoulder in uncertainty. "She is bat-shit crazy some times. Especially where I am concerned. Come to think of it, I haven't heard from her in a long time. It isn't like her to give up. Aggressive is her middle name."

"Well, there is no stench of her perfume. She is probably in the clear."

"Lexi ..."

The hairs on the back of her neck came up. Jason's tone suggested he was about to defend Annalise. Just when she was about to spout off, Christopher came back in, saving Jason from a volcanic eruption.

"I am going to my room," she said. "This will blow over. Good night."

"Good night, Lexi," Christopher said. "Everything is going to be fine. We will get a handle on this."

Lexi smiled and turned around to head for her bedroom. She looked down the hall to find Sadie and Stout lying at Jason's feet. Some days she wondered if they were her dogs or his. Deciding to leave well enough alone, she shut the door and walked over to sit on her bed. She bent her head and the tears began to spill. The evening had been a disaster. She had no business going on a date with Gage, or anyone else for that matter. Her heart belonged to someone else. Wiping the tears from her cheeks, she felt defeated.

What am I going to do?

She was in love with Jason and wanted no other. How could she move on if her heart didn't change course?

The next morning, as Lexi got ready for work, she heard a light tapping on her bedroom door.

"Lexi, it's Jason. Can we talk, please?"

She opened the door, staring at him with wet hair and black scrubs. Her eyes were puffy from crying and lack of sleep.

Jason's brow furrowed with concern. "Baby, are you all right?"

She was exhausted and didn't have the stamina to deal with him.

"Jason, what do you want?"

"I would like to take you to work today. It would really give me peace of mind. And I can bring you home. How about it?"

"Fine. I am almost ready."

"Good. That is good."

They sat next to each other in silence as Jason drove to the vet clinic. He knew that trying to communicate with Lexi at this moment was a bad idea. He wanted to fix things but could tell that the conversation would only lead to an argument. After pulling into the parking lot, he waited for Lexi to get into the building before he took off. She walked inside, waving good-bye. Jason thought he could see a slight smile as she did so, giving him hope for a reconciliation.

Jason stared at his computer screen. All he had seen for the last hour or so was a blur of colors. He couldn't concentrate. What he really wanted to do was storm into Gage's office and tell him to stay the hell away from Lexi. He leaned back in his chair, his hands supporting the back of his head. The more he thought about Gage and Lexi, the angrier he got. But losing his job was not in his best interest. *Keep your friends close and your enemies closer*. That is what he would do for the now.

The sound of his cell phone vibrating on the desk broke his train of thought. He opened a text from Lexi: "I am leaving work early for the day. I have a ride. Thank you."

What is up with that?

He pushed out of his chair and darted down the hall to Gage's office.

He stopped in the doorway to find that Gage was gone. This was too much of a coincidence. Lexi was going home and Gage was out of the office. He left the building as if he were running from a burning fire.

He *was* the fire. There would be no putting out these flames until he got his hands on Gage.

Jason pulled into the driveway and jumped out of the truck so fast he nearly forgot to put it in "park" and turn off the engine. Running into the house, he yelled for Lexi. But the house was still and quiet. Sadie and Stout were on the back porch scratching the sliding glass door forcibly. Something didn't feel right. He opened the door for the pups. They jumped and barked. He called out again for Lexi.

Sadie and Stout continued to bark, running toward the path leading to Mirror Pond. Jason followed, picking up the pace when he realized the dogs were leading him to something.

"Lexi Jane!"

No, not again. His heart raced, pumping adrenaline through his veins.

Sadie and Stout stopped at the edge of the pond, barking ferociously.

From a distance, Jason could see something floating in the pond. As he got closer, a sickening feeling overcame him. The object floating in the water was a body. Long strands of hair lay at the surface of the water.

"Lexi! God, no! Lexi!"

He ran past the terrified pups and dived headfirst into the water. When he reached the body, he grabbed hold of it and prayed he wasn't too late. He turned the body over and shrieked.

"Annalise. Jesus. What happened to you?"

He carried her body to land and pulled out his cell phone to dial 911.

"Shit. Come on."

The phone had suffered too much water penetration. It was dead. He threw it down and started chest compressions.

"Come on, Annalise. Come on."

From a distance, Jason could hear Lexi calling for Sadie and Stout. They took off immediately. Continuing chest compressions, he yelled at the top of his lungs through the thick forest.

"Lexi! Lexi, help!"

She heard his cry and took off as fast as she could.

"Jason! I'm coming."

"Hurry, Lexi!"

Her foot slipped on pine needles, causing her to fall. Her hands burned from scraping the palms against the sharp, dry needles. She shot back up to her feet and continued. As soon as she spotted Jason, she dropped to her knees beside him.

"Oh my God. What happened? Annalise?"

"Lexi, I need you to call 911."

The feeling of panic caused her hands to shake as she dialed.

"Someone has drowned at Mirror Pond," she said into the phone. "Please come quick. We are doing CPR."

She stayed on the line with the emergency services operator, covering the phone with her hand and looking at Annalise's limp body.

"Jason, what happened here?"

Maintaining the rhythm of the chest compressions, he was too winded to talk. Sirens sounded in the distance. Before long, Annalise was put onto an ambulance and pronounced dead.

"Jason, we need a statement from you," Officer Jenkins said. "Why don't we go up to the house?"

He escorted Lexi and Jason back to their house. Jason headed to his room to change into dry clothes. His body shook, nerves and chill taking over his system. When he sat down next to Lexi on the couch, she grabbed his hand and held it tight.

"I came home to check on Lexi," he said. "She told me she was coming home for the day. As you already know, we had an intruder in our house last night. The dogs were freaking out and led me to the pond, where I found Annalise. I don't know what happened to her. And, how did the dogs get out? Lexi always leaves them in. Something strange is going on, Officer."

Lexi squeezed Jason's hand. He was badly shaken up.

"You were involved with Annalise, romantically speaking?" the officer said.

Jason's eyes narrowed, glaring at Officer Jenkins with irritation. "You and I have known each other for years. Do you really think I would do something like this? We played football together ... We go back."

"I am simply gathering all of the facts, Jason."

"Annalise and I have hooked up in the past. A long time ago. She stops by and flirts. She wanted there to be more, but I didn't."

The officer pounded him with a few more questions.

"I will talk to you again soon, Jason. I can let myself out."

Lexi walked the officer to the door. Once he'd pulled out of the driveway, she walked over to Jason.

"Jason, I am so sorry."

He wrapped his arms around her, laying his head atop hers, and began to cry.

"I thought. I thought it was you, Lexi. Floating in the water. I have never felt so ..."

"Oh, Jason. It's all right. I'm fine. I am here for you."

He pulled out of her embrace and kissed her with urgent need. She held him tight, afraid to let go. The kiss ended to accommodate the release of more tears. She cried with him.

"I love you, Lexi."

Their foreheads touched and her hand stroked the side of his arm.

When her phone rang, she hesitated to walk away. She tried not let go of his hand as she looked to see who was calling.

"It's Christopher. I need to answer it and let him know what has happened."

Jason paced the living room, listening in on the conversation. When Lexi hung up, she looked at him with concern and empathy.

"Chris will be home later. He is tied up in Sunriver. "

She picked up Jason's hand and kissed the palm. He felt a tingle shoot through his entire body. Her hand held on to his as she led him to his room. Lexi unbuttoned his shirt and, with both hands, spread it open. She brushed her fingertips over his bare chest. She licked her lips before leaning in to place a gentle kiss on his flesh. He removed the shirt as she worked on the button and zipper to his pants. They dropped to the floor. Her fingers slipped into the waistband of his boxer briefs, pulling the soft cotton fabric down and over his erection. He sat on the bed, admiring the woman standing before him. Lexi released the hair tie holding her ponytail in place. Jason watched intently as she removed her black scrubs and shoes. Her breasts were confined by a red lace bra. She undid the strap and they plunged happily. Her nipples erect, she stood in front of Jason. His mouth took her breast while his hand cupped the side for support. Pulling him closer, she ran her hands through his hair. He continued sucking on her nipple as he worked on removing her panties. She assisted by stepping out of them so his mouth wouldn't leave her breast.

She pushed his shoulders back, encouraging him to lie down. She maneuvered herself on top of him, straddling her legs tightly against his body. She leaned down for a kiss, allowing him access to enter her. When she came back up, his shaft was inside her. He grabbed her hands, linking their fingers together. Her breasts danced before him as she pumped up and down his erection. She looked like a goddess, her wild mane draping everywhere. He released her hands to hold on to her hips. The pressure from his hands coerced her pelvis to plunge deeper, sending him over the edge. His orgasm exploded inside her. She stopped moving to feel him pulsate. His labored breathing slowed.

"Lay down next to me, Lexi."

Their bodies faced each other, legs intertwined. Jason kissed her, enjoying the feel of her tongue and the sweet taste. His hand moved up and down the curve of her bottom. She wanted to stay in this moment forever.

"Christopher will be home soon. We'd better get up."

Jason reached up her back to bring her in tighter, trapping her close to his body. "Don't move. You are not going anywhere. I will handle Christopher."

A vision of Annalise's body by the pond tapped into her head. "I can't believe Annalise is dead. Her poor family."

"Lexi, something shady is happening in our town. Right under our noses. Annalise didn't drown. Someone killed her and dumped her body." He wrapped his arms protectively around her. "Promise me you won't go down to the pond or out walking alone."

"Okay. I promise, Jason."

Jason's mind was processing. He had come home expecting to find Gage at the house with Lexi. Instead, he walked into a horror movie, finding Annalise dead. Where had Gage been? He shook the crazy thoughts away. What was he thinking? Gage ... a murderer?

He rolled over to hover above Lexi. His blue eyes focused on her hazel ones. His fingertips brushed the hair away from her forehead.

"Are you planning on seeing Gage again?"

"Is there any reason why I shouldn't, Jason?"

"You wicked sass. No more Gage."

If it had been any other man telling her what to do, she would have ignored the demand. But this was Jason being jealous, in control and proving to her that he was in. All in.

CHAPTER TEN

Burning Suspicions

The turmoil surrounding Annalise's death had the small town of Bend in a state of suspicion. Rumors and speculation as to who the killer was flooded the streets, heightening the fear. Jason had been called down to police headquarters on more than one occasion. He had strong alibis and was cleared as a suspect for the time being. On the last day of questioning, a disturbing coincidence was brought to his attention. The detective threw a picture onto the table in front of him.

"Do you recognize this vehicle, Jason?" the detective said, staring at him with intimidating eyes.

"I know someone with a car like that, but there are probably a dozen of them all over town, detective."

"This car was spotted in your neighborhood the night Alexis discovered there was an intruder in the house. The car belongs to Gage Phillips."

Jason shifted in his chair.

"Gage Phillips is your boss, correct?"

"Yes, sir."

"To your knowledge, did Mr. Phillips have any acquaintance with Annalise Gardner?"

Oh, crap. Things were heading in a bad direction.

"I introduced Annalise to Gage a while ago. He has never shared any information with me about dating her or ... You know, it doesn't mean anything."

"How about the fact that Mr. Phillips followed Alexis home after their date, possibly spying on her? Does that mean anything to you, Jason?" The detective's voice had gotten more serious and condescending.

"Hold on. This is allegedly. Maybe he just wanted to make sure she got home okay. I don't know."

"Did you see him at the office the day you found Annalise's body?"

"No. I had gone in, went straight to work and when I left, he wasn't in his office."

"Mr. Phillips is a suspect and you should take this seriously, Jason."

"All right. Understood."

Jason left the police station feeling like the wind had been knocked out of him.

Gage a suspect.

He pushed the ridiculous thought aside. But the fact that Gage had followed Lexi home after their date was disturbing. Could Lexi be the next victim?

He rubbed his hand over his face. *Shit. What am I doing? I have him guilty already, and as a serial killer no less.*

What was he supposed to do? This was crazy. Jason shook the thoughts away, pulled into work and went straight to his office. He shut the door behind him, booted up the computer and sat in the chair. He couldn't concentrate as he rocked and swiveled from side to side. Right at that moment, Gage knocked on his office door. Jason jumped and waved him in while trying to pull himself together.

"Hey, man, how are you holding up with everything?" Gage said. "Are the police still on your back? This is so absurd."

"Um, no. My alibis are legitimate and I am not considered a suspect. I really wasn't worried about it. I just needed to cooperate as much as possible."

"Right. Good. That is good."

Jason found it interesting that Gage didn't mention that he had been questioned as well and was officially considered a suspect. He probably wasn't aware the detective ratted him out, sharing all of the details, especially those pertaining to his following Lexi home. Jason stared at Gage, his mind spinning. What was going on in that head of his? "The killer is still loose out there. Why Annalise, you know? So many unanswered questions. Did she ever mention anyone strange to you, Gage?"

"No. We only hung out that one night after your party. She only talked about you."

Jason swallowed the lump in his throat. Thank God for alibis. "Listen, the other day I asked Alexis on a date and we went out. I know you wanted me to wait, but I did it anyway. Did she mention anything to you about it? I feel like the date didn't go very well, so I haven't reached out to her since. I think I screwed up."

Jason looked him in the eye curiously. *What does he mean by that?* "Yeah. I know the two of you went out. What makes you think you screwed up?" His foot tapped anxiously as he waited for Gage's response.

"I got too physical ... too fast. We started kissing and, oh man, I wanted her, you know?"

The image blew up inside Jason's head and fury detonated. He stood, pointing his finger right into Gage's face. "Lexi won't be seeing you anymore. Leave her alone."

Gage backed up, throwing his hands into the air. "All right. I guess it was a bad idea. This reaction is a bit extreme, don't you think?"

Jason dropped his hand and retreated behind his desk. "Just so we are clear, Gage."

Gage left the office quietly. Jason didn't know if he had awakened the beast or put him in hibernation. If Gage was the predator, would he lay low or pounce on his next prey?

"Alexis. Alexis!"

Olivia walked the halls of the vet clinic in a tizzy.

"There you are. Dr. Stephenson has to leave and wants me to put Henry away. I don't want to touch that slimy thing. Yuck."

"Well, what did you do with him in the meantime, Olivia?"

"I just left the filthy thing on the examination table."

"Really? Just to slither away and get lost in here somewhere? Jeez, Olivia."

Lexi ran down the hall and into the examination room, where she found Henry, a boa constrictor, stretched out against the side of the wall. Feeling a rush of relief, she picked him up and set him inside the glass terrarium.

"Well, do you see him in there?" Olivia called from the hall.

Lexi walked out of the room, counted to ten and pumped hand sanitizer into her hand. Rubbing the disinfectant all around, she thought of what to say to Olivia.

"I am at a loss for words."

"I know. I'm sorry, Alexis. Some animals aren't my thing, ya know?"

"Then why do you work in a vet clinic? I don't get it. You make me crazy sometimes."

"But you love me and would hate it if I wasn't here, Alexis. You know I'm right. You would be so bored without me. Come on ... admit it."

Lexi rolled her eyes and laughed. "It is getting late. Let's get out of here. Olivia, don't forget to take the pencils out of your hair before you leave."

Olivia pulled out one, two, three, four pencils and grabbed her purse before sprinting out the front door. Lexi finished cleaning up and left shortly after her. Walking out to her car, she looked up to admire the stars sparkling in the sky. It was dark out, but the stars shone bright like a streetlight just for her. She got to her Jeep and cringed.

"Oh, great. A flat tire. Not now."

She looked around the parking lot to see if anyone else was around.

"Shoot. Looks like I am the last one here. Well, should I suck it up and change this thing myself or call someone?"

She could hear tires in the dirt coming up behind her and she spun around.

"Oh shit. Hey, Gage. You scared me to death. What a relief it is you."

"Sorry, Alexis. I was driving by and saw you out here. I'm on my way home. Flat tire, huh?"

"Can you believe it? Your timing couldn't be better. Would you mind giving me a ride home?"

"Hop in. No problem at all."

His eyes followed her silhouette as she climbed into the front seat of the car.

"This is fancy, Gage. Leather seats and all. I bet you have seat heaters, too."

As Lexi rattled on, the only thing Gage could hear was Jason's voice telling him to stay away from her. He smiled at the thought of how pissed Jason would be right now. Passive aggressive? Who the fuck cared.

"I was hoping to get a chance to see you again, Alexis."

He glanced in her direction, noting that her attention was on her phone.

"Alexis?"

"Sorry, Gage. I just want to let Jason know what is going on."

Gage abruptly pulled the car to the side of the road. "What is it with you two? Do you have to report to each other over every single thing?"

Lexi's eyes opened wide. She was on high alert.

"I'm sorry. Is there a problem here, Gage? Maybe I should get out of the car now."

Gage leaned over her lap to keep her from opening the car door.

"No. No, don't go. I'm sorry. Please, let me take you home."

He pulled his arm back to the steering wheel and stared at the road in front of him. His hands twisted and turned around the wheel.

Lexi stared at Gage, wondering what was wrong with him. When her phone rang, Gage turned his head to see if she would answer.

"Hey, Jason. I had a flat tire. Gage is giving me a ride home. We are close."

She stared at Gage, daring him to do anything sketchy. After closing her phone, she kept watching him.

"Have you been to my house before, Gage? Seems you know where you are going."

Gage's heart sped up in panic. He'd screwed up. His mind raced to come up with a reasonable answer.

"Well, you know, I had to check out Jason's information. You all live together, right?"

Lexi's eyes narrowed in suspicion. That didn't sound right. She scooted even closer to the car door, ready to open it and jump out if need be.

Meanwhile, Jason ran out the front door to watch for Gage's car. Chris followed behind. Both men looked ready to brawl.

"Should we call the police?" Christopher said.

"Not until I get my hands on him first," Jason said. "Flat tire? How fucking convenient."

Gage came around the corner and pulled slowly into the drive.

Jason went straight for him. He reached into the open car window and had his hand around Gage's collar in a split second.

"Jason, stop," Lexi cried. "Please, stop. He didn't touch me."

He looked at Lexi's expression and let go of Gage. "Consider this my resignation, effective immediately." He pushed against Gage's chest and walked over to see Lexi out of the car. Christopher stood, keeping watch on Gage.

Lexi stepped out of the car and ran into the house as fast as possible.

Gage poked his head out of the car window. "You have got this all wrong, Jason. I was only trying to help."

"Get the fuck out of here, Gage," Christopher said.

He backed the car up and tore off down the street.

Jason found Lexi in the house, pacing the living room floor.

"We need to report this, Lexi. It is too weird. What are the odds that he would stumble upon you with a flat tire, late at night?"

She nodded. "I know. You're right. He didn't do anything to me, but there is definitely something off about him. Jason ... your job. I'm so sorry."

Jason wrapped his arms around her.

"Keeping you safe is all that I care about."

Gage arrived at his home, fury burning like an out–of-control brushfire.

He threw on gym clothes and headed for the basement. He grabbed a remote, turned on the Bose sound system and cranked up some heavy metal. He paused and then cranked the volume even more. He wasn't satisfied until his ears rang, distracting him from the voices in his head. He picked up a jump rope and wrapped the ends around each hand until there was no slack. Snarling, he pulled, snapped and twisted.

"Jason Walker doesn't know shit about me. Who does he think he is?"

One hand released the rope and he began slashing a black punching bag. As he whipped and thrust, sweat poured from his temples. He stepped back, throwing the jump rope to the floor. He picked up a terry towel and buried his face in it. Its rough texture scratched as his head moved from side to side. He rubbed the top of his head and the back of his neck with angry force.

After walking over to a cork board hanging from the red brick basement wall, he yanked a yellow Post-it note that was attached. He stared at the number on the small piece of paper.

"This isn't over. No way in hell."

CHAPTER ELEVEN

Mending the Line

The sun peeked through the blinds in Jason's room. He shifted his legs under the covers as he covered his eyes with the back of his hand. Lexi rolled over to drape her arm across his chest. Her leg covered his as she settled her head under his chin.

"Good morning." Jason said, with a groggy voice.

Lexi ran her fingertips through the curly brown hairs on his chest.

"Let's get away for the weekend," he said. "We could head over to Eugene and stay in one of those cabins overlooking the McKenzie River."

"Sounds nice. We can do some fly-fishing. I will grab the waders and rods and pack an ice chest."

Sadie and Stout were begging to go out.

"I need to let them out." She rolled on top of Jason, planting a kiss on his lips. He grabbed her buttocks, squeezing the soft flesh.

"Don't go. Stay here." He slipped his tongue inside her mouth.

Tasting him always did her in. He knew how to sway her decisions.

His hands moved up and down her bare back as she settled over his shaft. Then she took over, the power all in her movement. Her hands rested on his chest, arms taut, squeezing her breasts tightly together. Jason's arms lay above his head. His eyes never left the sight of her breasts, allowing her complete control as she chose the rhythm. Her arm moved around her back to reach down and stroke his testes.

"Good God," he said, breathing heavily.

Lexi pumped harder, maintaining grace and sexual poise. Jason's pelvis thrust toward Lexi one more time before he came inside her forcefully. His body shook and shivered.

She bent her head down close to his ear, her hair tickling his face as it fell forward. "I'm going to let the dogs out now. I will meet you in the shower. It is my turn, lover."

Jason smiled, more than thrilled to obey her orders. He watched as she threw on a robe and escorted Sadie and Stout out. He leaped off the bed, spotting Patches sleeping on his T-shirt. His brow furrowed as he noticed cat hair all over it.

I don't even care. I am way too happy to be upset.

He reached out to pet the soft feline. She lifted her head and let out a light kitty cry.

"See. There we go. We can get along."

He walked into the bathroom and eagerly turned on the shower. In a cloud of steam, he stood under the hot pounding pellets of water. He closed his eyes and rubbed his face.

Lexi walked into the bathroom, removed her robe and tossed it onto the tile floor. Opening the shower door, she admired the man in front of her. Water spray bounced off his body. She stepped inside and instantly bent down to place kisses across his lower torso. This area of his body turned her on. Her hands held on to his hips as she sucked on his flesh. He cupped the back of her head, remembering that it was her turn for pleasure.

"Lexi ..."

She stood to face him. Using his leg, he coaxed her legs apart, sliding his hand across her velvety tuft. He inserted a finger inside her, and without thought, she lifted her leg to allow better access. Jason kneeled down, draping Lexi's leg across his back. She felt the soft touch of his lips on her. His tongue explored, teasing her clit. She pressed her hands against the shower walls for support as he began sucking in an attempt to bring her to climax. Lexi began to feel lightheaded from the steam, her leg trembling as she orgasmed. She felt as though she could collapse from the intense pleasure. Jason released her leg and stood to hold on to her. His mouth landed on hers, their hands ravishing each other.

"If we don't stop, we will never get on the road, Jason."

"And the problem is?"

Lexi smiled. What was the rush anyway?

Christopher banged on Jason's bedroom door.

"Hey, man. I need you talk to you. I just got off the phone with Officer Jenkins."

"Hang on. Give me a second, Chris."

Jason threw on his jeans and headed out to the kitchen to find Christopher pacing around like a caged tiger. "What's going on?"

"A thorough background check has been done on Gage. They didn't find jack shit. No history of any criminal activity, mental illness or even porn."

"That doesn't mean he isn't coming off the hinges now. Shit. They probably won't get a search warrant. No probable cause."

Jason rubbed his chin, pondering the details. "Maybe we have been wrong about him. I mean, the thought did cross my mind that he might have something to do with all of this. But no other history ... It just doesn't add up. Criminals usually leave a trail behind them."

Lexi dragged the ice chest up the basement stairs, catching the end of their conversation. She set the chest down. "We are not wrong about him. You didn't see what I saw. He was agitated, disturbed. Everything you see out of a crime thriller. My gut says to stay clear of him."

"Did Officer Jenkins mention any new leads on Annalise?" Jason said.

Christopher looked at the ground, shuffled his feet and cleared his throat. "As of right now, they are leaning toward a fatal drowning. An accident. Knowing Annalise, she was probably drunk."

"She was in all of her damn clothes, Chris."

Christopher threw his arms into the air. "I don't know what else to say, Jason. It is what it is."

Lexi wrapped her arms around Jason, trying to distract him. "Come on. Let's get ready and head out of here."

Jason kissed the top of her head. He looked at Christopher with uncertainty. He wanted to believe that everything that had happened with Annalise and the intruder in their house was a fluke. It was hard to let it go.

"I will grab our bags."

Gage lay on his stomach. Pine needles poked through his thermal camouflage shirt. He adjusted the binoculars to get a clear view of the Taylor house. He picked up his cell phone and placed a call.

"Looks like they are going somewhere. They have duffel bags and an ice chest. Not sure about the brother. I can keep watch on him if you would like to proceed with your plans ... Roger that."

Using his elbows to maneuver and back up, he looked around to make sure the coast was clear before standing up. After wiping pine needles and debris from his pants, he climbed into his BMW, staring in a trance through the forest. He banged the dash with the side of his fist.

"Damn it! I'm in over my head."

He laid his head on the steering wheel, the palm of his hand continuing to bang the edge of the dash. The glove box caught his eye. He rubbed his palm where the redness and pain throbbed from the abuse it had taken. Leaning over to open the glove box, he retrieved a five-by-seven manila envelope. Staring at it, he contemplated how every wrong turn he made began with the contents inside. Burning it would protect him, leaving others ruined forever.

"Wow! Look at this place, Jason."

Lexi walked through the A-frame cabin, heading straight for the back. She opened the sliding glass door and stepped onto the wooden deck with two red Adirondack chairs and a picnic table with a red umbrella to match. Her mouth fell open at the view of the McKenzie River.

"The view of the river is amazing. Get out here. Hurry."

Jason dropped the duffel bags in the living room and admired Lexi as he approached. She wore her hair in a French braid that draped over the back of her yellow blouse. Her white shorts, frayed around the edges, led him to imagine what was underneath. He stood behind her, placing his hands on top of her shoulders.

"Pretty amazing," he said, bending his head down to kiss the side of her neck.

Goose bumps surfaced as she shivered from the feeling of the bristles of his beard brushing against her flesh. His arms dropped down to wrap around her waist. There were no words spoken as they listened to the sound of the water making its way downstream. A light breeze encouraged the Douglas fir trees to whisper. The river commanded their vision, their thoughts.

"Come on. Let's go do some fishing. This is too good to pass up."

"Bet my fish will be bigger than yours, Jason Walker."

"You are on!"

They ran into the house and out the front door to the truck to get their waders.

"Trout for dinner tonight, Jason. You can count on that."

In their waders, hiking down to the river posed a small challenge, but they got there. After stepping into the rushing stream, they walked across rocks to find the right pockets of water. They put some distance between them in order to compete. Game on. Feeling a bit rusty, Lexi concentrated on her casting technique, being careful not to let the fly line fall too low behind her. After a while, she heard Jason howl and looked over to see him reel in a shiny rainbow trout.

"Look at that beauty. Crap," she mumbled. "Focus, Lexi."

Her right arm continued the dance, careful not to flick her wrist. Her eyes intently watched the eddy, where she believed the fish to be lying in wait, ready to strike at a moment's notice.

"Come on. Come on."

She looked back to check on Jason and saw that he had gotten farther away from her. He smiled and waved.

"He is getting cocky on me," she said, laughing and shaking her head.

She worked her way farther down the river, stepping carefully on each stone. The pressure from the current began to increase against the back of her legs, nearly knocking her down. She stopped to catch her balance, looking behind for Jason, but he was out of sight. Feeling a bit uncomfortable, she decided to work her way toward the embankment. One step and balance. Next step, stop and balance. From the corner of her eye she saw movement through the trees.

"Jason? Hello? Who is out there?"

Her heart began to race as she continued her trek out of the water. The sound of footsteps on crunchy leaves caught her attention. She spun her head to look all around, moving her body in a complete circle. Securing the fly rod in her fist, she took off through the forest toward the cabin.

"Damn it, I can barely move in these waders."

She looked behind her to see if anyone was following. When she turned back around—*crash!* Jason grabbed her arms to keep her from falling to the ground. She hit his chest hard, sending her whole body backward.

"What's wrong? What happened?" he said, panicked.

Breathing too heavily to speak, Lexi used her finger to point in the direction of where she had been. Jason's eyes followed the direction of her finger, looking for something out of the ordinary.

"Some ... someone was out there," she said, gasping. "I could hear footsteps behind me."

"Are you sure, Lexi? Could it have been an animal?"

"I don't ... I guess, maybe. It freaked me out."

"I've got you. It's okay." He put his arm around her shoulder and guided them back to the cabin. "Hey, I have two beautiful trout for us. Not trying to rub it in or anything."

Lexi smiled, calming down by the moment. She looked behind them. Someone had been watching her. Following her. *I am not crazy.*

They climbed out of their waders, left them by the front door and leaned the fly rods against the wall.

"I am going to go clean the fish," Jason said. "I will be back in a minute."

After lingering in the doorway for a moment, hesitant to go in without Jason, Lexi filled a teapot with water, set it on the stove and lit the fire. Leaning against the counter, she tapped her fingers nervously. Everything that happened, the break-in and the murder, was messing with her, causing paranoia. Anxiety built up in her bloodstream, causing her heart to flutter. She began rummaging through the kitchen cupboards and found the perfect remedy.

"Forget tea—bring on the whiskey!"

She found a small glass and gave herself a generous poor. She lifted the glass to her nose, closed her eyes and inhaled the intense aroma. Hints of smoke and caramel alerted her senses. The moment the golden tonic hit her lips, she could feel the burn that would soon be in the back of her throat. She let it sit on her tongue before swallowing, allowing the flavor to build. There was a moment of silence, distraction and pleasure. Then the whistling of the teapot caused her eyes to pop open, ruining the moment. She turned off the burner, set the pot aside and took her whiskey into the living room.

"What is taking Jason so long?" she mumbled, looking out the window.

The sun was going down and the air had turned chilly. The wind began to pick up, causing the umbrella on the patio to turn into a sail. Lexi could see from inside that it would break or blow over. She set her glass down and rushed outside to retrieve the umbrella. The wind blew her hair in every direction, and she could feel water spray from the river. She grabbed on to the pole and pulled as hard as she could to get it out of its hole. When it finally gave, the wind knocked her to the ground. She scrambled to her knees to close up the umbrella and tucked it under the picnic table. She stood, brushed off her knees and looked up at the sky. Clouds had developed, moving across the sky swiftly. She rubbed her arms to fight off the chill, and when she turned around to go back in the house, she was startled by a silhouette standing in the back door.

"Jesus, Jason, you scared me," she said, stepping closer. "You look like you have been cleaning up a crime scene or something. Look at your shirt, and is that fish guts splattered across your face?"

Jason smiled, holding up two gutted fish. There was a time when he refused to gut and clean any of the fish they caught. Christopher and Lexi were always stuck with the task.

"You are looking pretty pleased with yourself. I see you got over your guilt about the fish biting the hooks."

"Let's fire up the grill."

Lexi reached up to take the fish. "I will take care of these. You might want to go take a shower, Jason."

Jason whistled a tune as he dried off his body with a towel.

"Man, I love a hot shower." Rubbing his hair with the towel, he stepped out of the bathroom and into the living room, exposing every inch of his flesh. "My mouth is watering, I can already taste the trout." He dropped the towel, looking around the living room. "Lexi?"

Peeking his head outside, he noticed the fish on the ground near the grill. He stepped out onto the patio, bare butt and all, his eyes searching.

"Lexi! Lexi, where are you?"

All he could hear was the sound of the river, the water moving rapidly downstream and splashing the rocks. He picked up the fish, noticing that the grill was lit, both sides on "high."

"Where did she go? Shit." He tossed the fish into the trash can and turned off the grill.

He ran into the house, opened the front door and hollered her name several times. No response. He slammed the front door shut and rushed into the bedroom to get his cell phone off the nightstand. After dialing Lexi, he balanced the phone between his ear and shoulder as he pulled jeans over his legs and secured the button at the waist.

"Voice mail. Shit!"

He tossed the phone onto the bed and grabbed a T-shirt from his duffel bag. From the corner of his eye he spotted Lexi's purse. He emptied the contents onto the bed. The first item to fall out was her Glock.

"Lexi Jane. Where are you?"

He slid the Glock into his back packet. One more search around the property. After retrieving a flashlight from his pickup, he walked down the wooden steps around the side of the house toward the river. It was a dark night, with little to no moon to help guide his way. The wind howled, blowing leaves in every direction. He shone the flashlight through the trees, down the path and across rocks to catch any possible clues. He stood at the edge of the river, listening intently, his flashlight scanning the area like a spotlight. He cupped his hand around the side of his mouth to create an echo.

"Lexi! Lexi!"

He looked downstream as a horrid vision of her floating down the river drifted through his mind. Panic built up, telling him it was time. He pulled out his phone and dialed 911.

CHAPTER TWELVE

Saving Lexi

Lexi tried desperately to open her eyes. Feeling as though she were in the middle of a heavy dream, she struggled. Extreme brain fog clouded her ability to function. With urgency, her mind kept telling her to wake up. Her head moved from side to side, and she could feel her eyes rolling around inside their sockets. Slowly, one eye opened and then the other followed. As she tried to swallow, there was barely enough saliva to allow it. She cringed at the dry and sore feeling coming from the back of her throat. A throbbing pain pounded the top of her head. Her hand reached up to touch it.

What is going on? Where am I?

She tried to remember what happened. The pounding headache, delaying her memory, wasn't helping. The floor she lay on felt hard. It wasn't cold like concrete. Rubbing her hands against it, she felt grit and realized it was the texture and smell of wood. As the minutes went by, the darkness turned to light. She could hear muffled voices nearby but could not make out a word. She looked around the large room in an effort to identify her surroundings. She rolled her body over in an attempt to stand up. Everything was a blur, her equilibrium completely thrown off. Her hand located a wall, allowing her to scoot her back up against it. It felt rough, splinters of wood snagging her hair.

She identified several small windows near the top of the ceiling that admitted some light. The room smelled musty, as if it had been closed up for a while. She could see dust hovering like a cloud through the rays of natural light. Feeling around the pockets of her shorts, she tried to find her phone.

"Damn it."

Her memory began to slowly come back to life. She thought of the cabin in Eugene.

"Fish. I was about to cook our fish. Jason ..."

Her heart started pumping rapidly. The blood flow heightened her awareness, clearing the fog that had taken over her brain. Fear turned on the adrenaline like a sharp needle to the chest. Using the wall to brace herself, she stood up. Looking down at her feet, she realized she had no shoes on. She circled the room to investigate, hoping to find a way out or an item to protect herself with. It was a much bigger space than she'd realized.

"What is this place?"

There were old wooden conveyor belts. She realized the grit she felt on the floor was sawdust. Exploring further, she discovered a large metal saw at the end of the belt. After spotting a door, she ran over to it. It was a sliding barn door that wouldn't budge. Lexi bent her knees, pulling the door with all her force, trying desperately to open it.

"Ugh ... come on!"

She heard horns from a train spouting off nearby. Recognizing it, she felt relieved to know she wasn't far from home. She paced the room trying to remember who took her and how. She had no recollection of seeing a face or talking to anyone other than Jason. Wishing she could reach one of the windows, she looked around for a ladder. Something that would get her up there. Maybe she could get a clue to her whereabouts and yell for someone. She looked to the ceiling and around the room. Finding herself discouraged, she realized there wasn't anything to boost her up to the windows. No tools for protection. Just sawdust, walls and conveyor belts.

Nausea built up in her stomach as chills rolled through her body. She wondered what would happen to her. Would she end up like Annalise? The next target and victim. Her head snapped around as she heard footsteps approaching. She ran behind the conveyor belt and stared at the door as the lock jiggled and the door slid open. As the person entered the room, Lexi's eyes popped wide open. She grabbed her stomach, vomiting all over the floor. Her knees felt like they would buckle at any moment.

"That wasn't a very nice greeting, Lexi. Good to see you, too."

* * *

"Christopher, you are not the law," Officer Jenkins said. "What were you thinking going over to Gage Phillips's place causing an uproar like that? He could press charges and has every right."

"I needed to know if he was home or not. If he had any part of Lexi's disappearance."

"That is our job, Chris. You barged into his house and threatened him. We have teams out looking for her. You just be here for Jason. Did you get a hold of Dr. Stephenson and Olivia?"

"Yes."

"Stay away from Mr. Phillips. Got that? We will find her, Chris."

"She sure as hell better not end up like Annalise."

Jason came barreling through the front door. After being up all night with police in Eugene, he was amped and on a tear.

"I am taking Sadie and Stout back to the cabin in Eugene. Maybe they can lead us to something."

"Jason, they aren't tracking dogs," Christopher said.

"Do you have a better idea, Chris? I can't sit around and do nothing."

Christopher looked at Officer Jenkins. "I heard what you said. Keep us posted. Jason and I need some time."

The officer hesitated, suspicious that Christopher had something up his sleeve. But then he waved and left the house.

Christopher turned to Jason.

"We are on our own, man. I have a plan. Tonight, we go out." Chris said.

Jason took Sadie and Stout out to search up and down the Deschutes River, hoping for any sign of Lexi's whereabouts. Annalise had been dumped at Mirror Pond. Maybe the son of a bitch had a pattern. He stopped to stare at the river, and a realization burst in his brain like an aneurysm, sending shockwaves through his system. Both victims were women he was associated with. It was all beginning to feel personal. Of all places to dump Annalise, they chose the one location where he spent most of his time growing up. A place close to his heart. So many years of good memories.

What the hell? This is someone we know.

He put the dogs on their leashes and headed quickly back to the house. He ran up the back steps with eager determination and rushed inside.

"Christopher!"

They nearly slammed into each other as they met at the end of the hall.

"What is it?"

Jason grabbed on to Christopher's shoulders, looking him square in the eye. "We know him."

"Who? What are you talking about? Slow down."

"Whoever has Lexi is someone we know, Chris. And they are trying to get to me. Warn me, hurt me. I am sure of it. Think about it. Annalise and Lexi. Mirror Pond? It is all too fucking coincidental."

"All right. But who, Jason? And why? What have you ever done to anybody?"

"I just feel it. She is going to be dead if we don't figure this out. No waiting until dark. We start with our plan now!"

Lexi stared in shock at the man standing before her. She tried to process what was happening. She cleared her throat, but still not a word would come out.

"What? Looks like I have you all choked up, Lexi Jane Taylor. Surprised to see me? Ha, ha, ha."

She backed up against the wall, the stench from her vomit causing more nausea.

"What a mess. Disgusting. So dramatic, Lexi."

The man shook his head in distaste. She watched him walk over to a workbench, pull a towel out of a drawer and throw it directly at her. Lexi made no effort to catch it, allowing the towel to land on the ground.

"Pick that up and clean up your mess."

Lexi slowly bent down to retrieve the towel, her eyes never leaving his. The courage to speak finally made its way through her voice box.

"I don't understand. Where have you been and why are you doing this? Did you kill Annalise?"

"It had to be done. She would have trapped Jason with a pregnancy. Spiteful, deceitful. Never liked that girl. She has been trouble since day one."

Lexi's heart wrenched, remembering how Annalise lay dead on the side of the pond. "Why did you dump her in Mirror Pond? Why not bury her or burn the body?"

"Where's the fun in it all if you don't make it dramatic?" he said, grinning from ear to ear.

Lexi swallowed, wondering how she was going to get out of this situation. She was there for a reason. She looked at the faded towel with holes throughout. It had been eaten away by moths. Keeping a close eye, Lexi bent down to wipe up the chunky particles.

"What is it with you women? You just screw us over. You and Jason will never happen and I will make sure of it."

Lexi shuffled back closer to the wall, throwing the towel at his feet. Wiping her hands on the back of her shorts, she plotted her next move. She had to prepare to fight. Any way she could. The man looked down at the towel.

"You have always been such a handful. Can't you ever just behave instead of challenging people all the goddamned time? What is wrong with you, child?"

"In case you haven't noticed, I'm no longer a child or afraid of you."

He tried to be dominant, but all Lexi saw was a tired, bitter old man. He had aged significantly over the years, looking weathered and crusty.

By the looks of his gray hair and beard, it didn't seem he had taken a shower in quite a while. The same destructive man in the body of someone who didn't take care of himself.

He may have gotten me here, but I can take him now.

* * *

"Listen, we can get in a lot of trouble for this," Christopher said. "Last chance to back out."

"If Lexi winds up dead, I won't give a shit if I go to jail. Let's do this."

Jason took a crow bar and broke the window out of Gage's BMW. After unlocking the door, he crawled inside to begin his search.

"I'm going up to the house," Christopher said. "I will get Gage to talk."

He walked to the front door and banged on it as he tried to let himself in. The door was locked. He peeked inside the front window and saw someone move swiftly.

"He is going to run, Jason! I am going around the house. You watch for him out here."

Christopher spotted Gage running out the back and took off after him. Gage hopped the back fence in one stealthy movement. Chris followed, tracking closely as he tried to catch up to him. His feet moved faster and faster. Determination turned up his pace. He was close enough to grab the back of Gage's shirt. His fingers latched on and he pulled Gage to the ground. Christopher landed on top of him, straddling him like a wrestler to keep him from moving. He grabbed his throat and pushed his head securely to the ground.

"You are going to talk and tell us everything. You hear me?"

Gage's eyes bulged, his legs kicking.

Jason watched out the car window as he foraged through the console. Nothing but a pair of Ray-Ban sunglasses and loose coins. Feeling under the driver's seat, he spotted the glove box. When he opened it, a pile of papers, napkins and a manila envelope fell out. Keeping watch for Gage, he rummaged through the papers. Car insurance, registration, all that bullshit. He picked up the manila envelope, his hands trembling. Tearing it open at the top, he felt the sting from a paper cut. He stared in amazement as he went through every item inside. There were numerous photos of himself, Lexi and Annalise. Christopher was present in some, but the focus had clearly been on the others. They had all been watched and followed. The last piece of paper displayed a note. The signature jumped out at Jason like a scary clown. Only it wasn't a clown—it was a ghost.

"Oh my God. No fucking way."

Feeling himself go flush, he pulled out his phone.

"Officer Jenkins, I know who has Lexi. It is Billy Walker. My father has Lexi."

CHAPTER THIRTEEN

Walker vs. Taylor

Lexi tried to recall the last time she had seen Billy Walker. It was never a pleasant event. Between the depression and the alcohol abuse, the Taylors chose to steer clear. Over the years, Mirror Pond had been the safe haven for the threesome. Fishing, swimming and snowball fights were just a few of the activities they'd engaged in there over the years. For a few hours each day, Jason could forget about the sadness within the walls of his home, spending time with people who truly cared about him. She watched as Billy paced the room.

"Mr. Walker, I love Jason. I always have."

He laughed sarcastically, shaking his head. "You and your family. Always up in our business, acting like you are better than us. Brainwashing Jason so that he didn't want to be in his own damn home."

"Is that how you see it? You might want to have a sit-down with your son and ask him how he remembers his home life."

Lexi could see the rage build in his gray eyes.

"The second your parents died, Jason didn't hesitate to move in. You filled his head with guilt and pressure. Lexi Jane Taylor always full of spit and vinegar, tangling my son in all the bad crap you did."

Lexi could feel the tension build even more. The building turned into a very small space in a matter of seconds.

"I have waited a long time to say these things to you. For years I have thought about the Taylors. All high and mighty."

Lexi wanted nothing more than to lay into him and tell him how the real story went. If she had any hope of getting out of this alive, challenging him was not the way to go. She maintained her guard, biting her tongue and plotting her survival.

"You sure grew up to be a pretty thing, though. I will give Jason that. I would want to get inside those pants, too. I bet he already has. He has, hasn't he? The Walker men have a way of getting the ladies."

That was it. Lexi couldn't hold back another second.

"You are disgusting. Don't ever compare yourself to Jason. He is nothing like you. He may carry your name, but that is all the Walker he is, you son of a bitch."

Billy smiled, walking toward her.

"Do not underestimate what I will do to you if you touch me, Billy."

Licking his lips, he reached out to grab her arm. She pushed him in the chest, causing him to stumble backward. He rubbed his chin, glaring deep into her eyes with fury. Lunging at her, he caught hold of both her arms. Lexi kneed him in the balls and stomped the top of his foot. If only she had been wearing her stilettos. He gasped, bending over to grab his junk.

Lexi ran toward the barn door. Billy dived to the ground, grabbing her ankle and sending her crashing to the floor. She quickly rolled onto her back and kicked him in the chest as he tried to hover above her. Scooting backward, she got up off the floor, dodging his next advance. She had to stay ahead of him. He was on his feet, and she danced around him, ready to pounce.

"You stupid bitch. We both know how this ends."

Lexi didn't respond. There was a huge advantage to growing up with boys. Christopher and Jason taught her to wrestle, shoot pistols and street-fight. Billy went straight for her throat with his bare hands. Her arm came up and she thrust the palm of her hand under his nose with force. He staggered, giving her time to punch him on the side of the face.

Down he went. Shaking the pain out of her hand, she made another attempt for the door. She pulled with all her might to get the heavy barn door to move, maneuvering it just enough to squeeze through. She ran but immediately tripped on a block of foundation and fell to the ground. After getting back up, she took off like a bat out of hell. Recognizing her surroundings as she trekked through tall weeds and brush, she headed straight for the main road. She looked behind her to see if Billy was on her tail.

Don't look behind you. Don't look. Keep going.

She ran faster.

"They are not at the old Walker house," Officer Jenkins said. "The current residents are home and we have searched the entire place. Where else would Billy take her? Can you think of any place he used to hang out or talk about?" He looked directly at Jason.

"Gage must know. Offer him a deal. Some incentive to rat Billy out."

"The boys at the station are doing everything they can. He is not cooperating."

"You should have let me have him, Jenkins," Christopher said. "I would have gotten it out of him."

"You almost choked him to death, Chris. What good would that have done?"

"I haven't thought about my father in years," Jason said. "He has been dead to me. I don't know. He spent every hour of every waking day rocking back and forth in that damn recliner, staring at a fuzzy TV screen. He never went anywhere. Certainly didn't have any friends that I can recall." He looked at Christopher, his eyes pleading for him to come up with something.

"Billy never took you to a storage unit or a special place to hunt, shoot guns? Anything like that?"

Jason rubbed his hands over his face. He was about to explode.

"Think, Jason."

Tears began to stream down his face. "I am thinking as hard as I can. Time is running out. We shouldn't just be sitting here."

"Jason, didn't Billy do some work over at the old mill years ago?" Christopher said.

"Yeah, so? Being it is a shopping and dining area now, I don't see where he would take her. They would be completely exposed."

"The other building, Jason. Mill A, on the opposite side of the river. The building needs renovation, and as far as I know, it is unoccupied."

Jason looked at Officer Jenkins. "That could be it. Let's get out there. Now!"

"I will send a team out to meet us."

* * *

The bottom of Lexi's feet burned from the scraping of rocks and debris, but she kept moving, ignoring the discomfort. Adrenaline kept her moving like a freight train. In the distance, she heard a truck engine fire up. She didn't want to get off the main road, hoping and praying someone would come along before Billy. The sound of the truck's muffler got louder, alerting her that he was almost on her. She was about to lunge down toward the river when she saw headlights coming right at her. Waving her arms in the air, she could see emergency vehicle lights flashing.

Keep going, Lexi. Don't stop ... Don't stop.

Billy revved the engine, his speed accelerating. He focused on Lexi with the intent of running her over. When she darted to the side of the road, the truck and two police cars slammed on their brakes, nearly colliding with each other.

"There she is. That's Lexi!" Jason yelled. "Hurry, Christopher. Catch up to her."

Lexi looked behind her to see what was happening. Billy was armed, the police taking cover at their vehicles. Sirens sounded in the distance—back up on its way. She spotted Christopher's truck and Jason high-tailing it to reach her. She flew into his arms, nearly out of breath, and latched on with the force of a vise.

"Lexi. God, baby. Come on. Let's get you into the truck and out of here."

She took his hand and followed quickly behind. Christopher hopped back into the truck to get them the hell out of there. Lexi slid across the seat and hugged her brother, her whole body shaking with fear.

"It's okay. You are okay," Christopher said, holding on tight.

"Jason. Your dad. It's bad. He killed Annalise. He would have killed me, too, if I hadn't..."

Jason put his arm around her, securing her tightly next to him. "It's over now. We've got you."

She looked at him and her heart ached. As if he hadn't been through enough growing up. Now this. What would it do to him?

Several more police cars approached with a vengeance, and gunshots were fired. Screeching his tires, Christopher backed the truck up as fast as he could and tore out onto the road. Punching the accelerator, they tore down the street, leaving a cloud of dust in their tracks.

There was nothing but silence inside the pickup for a few miles. Lexi's feet burned with pain. Lifting one up, she examined the damage.

"Lexi, that looks bad," Jason said. "Let me see the other one." He examined the other foot. "Shit, Chris. Let's go straight to the hospital."

"I can take care of this at home, Jason," Lexi said.

"Your feet could get infected. You should be checked out all over." He paused, treading carefully before getting into the details. "Did Billy ... Did he hurt you or touch you in any way?" He was not completely sure he was ready to hear the answer.

Christopher looked at Lexi, waiting for a response.

"He tried. I got away. You guys raised me right."

Flooded with relief, Jason and Christopher burst out laughing, knowing full well that Lexi could beat up most any guy who came along. A real Ronda Rousey—badass and beautiful.

"Look out when you mess with Lexi Jane Taylor," Christopher said.

Lexi's smile faded as she thought about what had happened before they left the road to the old building. "I hope no one was killed. We should try calling Officer Jenkins."

Christopher pulled into the ER entrance and Jason hopped out of the truck, offering his hand to Lexi. When she scooted closer, he picked her up and carried her inside. Several nurses came toward them.

"Oh my gosh, Lexi!" Janice the nurse said. "Everyone has been looking for you. Thank God you are okay. Small town—everyone knows about it. Let's get you checked in. The buzz around here has been unreal."

Jason set Lexi down in a wheelchair. His hands rested on the arms of the chair as he looked into her eyes. "I will come back there when they say it's okay. I will just be in the way right now."

Lexi smiled, the desire to kiss him nudging her.

"I would kiss you, Jason, but I strongly recommend that doesn't happen right now. Long story."

Nurse Janice pulled the wheelchair back, separating the two lovebirds.

Jason couldn't take his eyes off Lexi. His heart ached as the sick feeling in his stomach swirled at the thought of her being dead. She could have easily ended up like Annalise. She probably would have if it weren't for her tomboy ways.

His phone buzzed and vibrated, snapping him out of his morbid thoughts. Officer Jenkins's name came up on the screen.

"Hey. I am at the hospital with Lexi. What happened out there? We heard the gunshots. Is everyone okay?"

"Jason, Billy gave us no choice but to fire our weapons. He was the only casualty. I am so sorry. I can't imagine how you must feel."

Silence lingered in the air.

"Jason?"

"It's okay. He is off the streets. The threat to our town and loved ones has been eliminated. What about Gage?"

"Gage has been arrested. He will be tried as an accomplice, thanks to the contents in that envelope you found. Only problem is, the evidence could get thrown out due to the way it was recovered. You catch my drift?"

"We did what we had to do," Jason said.

"I need you to go down to the morgue. You need to identify Billy and let the mortician know what you want done with the body."

"Let's get it over with."

Jason slammed his phone shut. Rubbing his forehead, he walked over to Christopher, who was hanging out in the waiting room.

"My dad is dead. I have to go."

CHAPTER FOURTEEN

Because I Love You

"Autumn shows us how beautiful it is to let things go."
– Unknown

Lexi walked out to the back porch, steam rising from her cup of joe. Wrapping a fleece blanket around her shoulders, she sat in the wooden swing that had been neglected over the years. Hinges in dire need of oil creaked as she began to rock. She found the sound charming, for somehow it melded with the crisp fall air. Her fingers slid across the seat, sharp pricks from the weathered wood surprising her. She turned the palm of her hand over to make sure there were no splinters. An afternoon of staining would be a nice project on a day like this. Looking into the forest, she turned her attention to the changing colors of the leaves. She missed the rock chucks grazing the land before hibernation. A gentle breeze shuffled leaves across the ground as tree branches danced to the song it played. As Lexi listened, she heard a low humming sound and an occasional whistle streaming through the air, making her eyes believe she could see the air move in front of her.

Taking a sip of her coffee, she could feel the warm liquid travel all the way down to her stomach. Snuggling deeper into the blanket, she crossed her ankles, preparing to stay a while. She reflected on the events of the summer, thankful it was all behind her. Still, the lingering effect it had on herself and Jason left her feeling melancholy. She wanted to bury the memory, moving forward to a positive future.

Annalise's funeral had been a sorrowful event. It brought on a tremendous amount of guilt for Lexi. It seemed so disrespectful to even be there, knowing that Annalise had been her least favorite person. Her parents so distraught. Losing a child was something no one could possibly recover from. It would change a person forever. And then, Jason ...

* * *

Lexi tapped on Jason's bedroom door.

"Jason? Can I come in?"

She gently nudged the door open and peeked inside. He sat in the nook of the bay window, looking out to nowhere.

"Hey. Are you hungry?" she said. "Can I make you anything?"

Jason shook his head. "No, Lexi. Come over here and sit down."

The remnants of sadness had been etched all over his face since Billy's death. Jason had dealt with every emotion possible, completely haunted by his father's actions. Past and present. Lexi feared that Jason would be scarred forever.

"I have been doing a lot of thinking, Lexi. I love you. More than you could possibly know. I do. Please believe me. But I need to get out of here. I don't think I can shake this unless I leave town for a while." He picked up her hand, holding it tightly. Looking into her eyes, he pleaded for support.

"Where will you go?" she said, trying to muffle the crack in her voice.

"Back to Seattle. There is a lot of work for me there. And, it is far away from here."

Tears pooled in her eyes and fell down her cheeks. Jason reached up to swipe them before they could drop, the lingering question in the air still unanswered.

"I love you, Jason. I will support you no matter what. You have been through so much. Where does this leave us? On hold or ..."

"I need time, Lexi. I don't expect you to wait for me."

Her mind begged her not to fall apart, but her heart took over. She fell into his arms, sobbing. Her hand pulled on his T-shirt while her head lay on his shoulder.

"I'm so sorry, Lexi. This has nothing to do with you. I don't want to be here, and coming with me isn't an option. Not right now."

She pulled away, wiped the tears and stood to get herself together. "Do what you need to do, Jason. Please, let me know when you are leaving. Don't leave without saying good-bye. Give me at least that."

He nodded. The sooner he left, the better for everyone. "I'm leaving this afternoon, Lexi."

Feeling as though she had been knocked over, she gathered herself to respond.

He walked over to her. Picking up both her hands, he looked deep into her hazel eyes, begging for forgiveness. "I think we should say good-bye now. It's not forever, you know?"

Lexi was at a loss for words. After everything they had been through, she had truly believed Jason would stay by her side this time. She knew he was struggling emotionally, and she longed to help him through it. Turned out, her help wasn't what he needed. Time apart was. The reality: he was running from the pain, the embarrassment and anything that had to do with Billy Walker.

Jason bent his head down to kiss her, and their lips locked passionately. Passion turned to desperation as her arms came around to hold him tight, longing to not let go. He stroked her back, pulling her in as close as he could. The intensity began to subside, as they knew the kiss had to end sooner than later. Lexi stepped away from Jason, her eyes stuck on his as she opened the door. She paused in the doorway for one last look.

"Take care, Jason. You always have a home here. My heart will always belong to you."

Jason felt a sharp pain shoot right through him.

"Good-bye, Lexi Jane."

* * *

A red-tailed hawk flew past Lexi, snapping her out the heart-wrenching memory. A small bird flapped its wings in double time to escape the grasp of the swift talons. She watched on, hoping the little guy would get away. Nature was a dynamic, peculiar thing, she thought. Birds after other birds, fish eating other fish. People hurt other people. Humans and animals weren't all that different in many ways.

Not a day had gone by that Lexi didn't think of Jason. There was an occasional sad, awkward phone call from time to time. Lexi disciplined herself, as hard as it was, to leave him alone. Space was his medicine, his therapy. She couldn't bear to deny him anything that would heal his heart and soul. She got up to go back into the house, dragging the fleece blanket with her. She fumbled inside an old desk for paper and a pen and sat down at the kitchen table. She stared into space to gather her thoughts before she could begin.

Dear Jason,

It is with sincere love that I am writing to you, hoping this letter finds you in good health, both mentally and physically. I could not allow the time to pass without sharing with you, most deeply, that I recognize how crucial this time is for you. Having said that, it is equally as important to me to tell you that there isn't a day that goes by I don't think of you and miss you with all my heart. It is my greatest desire that you will recover from all of the inflicted pain and find your way back to the ones who love you most dearly, without judgment or anger.

All my love, now and forever

Lexi Jane

Lexi stuffed and sealed the envelope and took the letter straight to the mailbox. Hoping the letter wasn't a subconscious effort to manipulate him, she shut the door and pulled the red flag up. Her instincts told her it was the right thing to do. Putting her feelings down on paper in an honest and loving way had been a form of therapy for her. An outreach, with no pressure or guilt.

Sadie and Stout were pressing their noses against the screen door, anxiously waiting for Lexi's return. She smiled, feeling thankful for her loyal pups. They would get her through this challenging time. Life had to move on, with or without Jason Walker.

Several weeks later, Lexi decided it was time to participate in an activity other than going to work and walking the dogs.

"Hey, Christopher. I was thinking a drive up to Sisters sounded nice. What do you think? You up for it?"

"Lexi, I have been meaning to talk you about something. I would love to go, but, um, I have a date tonight."

"You do? Who is it, Chris?"

"We have been on more than a few dates, Lexi. I should have told you sooner. I didn't want to make a big deal out of it, you know, in case things weren't working out. I'm really happy. Feels different. Even better, she isn't from around here. She is new to the area. Her name is Sutton."

Lexi smiled, patting her brother on the arm. "That is great, Chris. I'm so happy for you. We could all go together. It would be a nice easy way to get to know each other. I would love to meet her. If you are ready."

"All right. I will run it by her, but I'm sure she will be fine with it."

Lexi laughed. "I can handle being a third wheel. Besides, I need to check this girl out. Make sure she is right for you."

"Uh, Lexi ..." Christopher said, frowning with concern.

"Relax, I am only teasing. I will be on my best behavior. I promise."

"No packing the Glock today, okay? Maybe it's time to lock it back up."

Lexi was reluctant to comply. Ever since the abduction, her Glock had been a permanent fixture on her body. But Dr. Stephenson put his foot down at the clinic, asking her not to bring it to work in his jolly, sweet way. Maybe she needed to give it a rest for a while. Lock it back up.

Strolling into her room, she stared at her purse. Keeping the gun close had been her safety net, her peace of mind. She opened the handbag, extracted the Glock and stepped inside her closet to lock it up. No more crutches.

"You never know how strong you are... until being strong is the *only* choice you have" – Bob Marley

CHAPTER FIFTEEN

Delusional Measures

The sound of a ruckus coming from the living room brought Christopher out of a state of sleeping bliss. Most of his workdays consisted of waking up before dawn and using every second of daylight. This particular Saturday morning, he had been determined not to crawl out of bed until the sun was up. Winter was on the brink of emerging, holding the light at bay a while longer.

"Good grief. What is Lexi doing out there?"

Groaning, he rolled out of bed and pulled on plaid pajama bottoms. He rubbed his tired eyes and ventured out to investigate.

He found Lexi in the kitchen washing dishes. She was bright-eyed and had a bounce in her step. Dressed in black leggings and a knee-length gray sweater covering a white blouse, she flitted around on a mission.

"You are up and raring to go. What's got you on fire this morning?" He walked over to the coffee pot, grabbed a large mug from the cupboard and he poured the black liquid to the rim.

Lexi dried her hands and draped the dish towel over the sink. "I'm going to Seattle, Chris. I'm bringing Jason home."

Christopher choked, spitting hot coffee and inhaling a bit through his nostrils. "What? Are you sure you want to do that, Lexi? Have you even heard from him?"

Lexi looked down at the ground, fighting the urge to chicken out on her plans. "It is time, Christopher. It has been months since he left. His home is here, with us. We have done everything he asked. We have stayed away, left him alone. Enough is enough."

Christopher squeezed her arm gently. "What if he doesn't want to come back, Lexi? Are you prepared for that?"

She looked into the distance, searching her heart for the answer.

"I, uh ... I can't think about that. I have to try, Chris. Please don't talk me out of this."

"Why don't I come with you? The odds are better if we both go. Not to gang up on him, just to remind him of what he left behind. Come on, what do you think?"

"I think I have to do this on my own. I want him to come home because he wants a life with me. I can't take this anymore. Actions speak louder than words. I don't want to be in a relationship with someone who runs away every time there is a crisis. He is in, or he is out."

"Lexi, I don't disagree that you have been more than patient and have gone above and beyond in this situation. I worry about how it will affect you if things don't go the way you are hoping they will."

She put her hands on her hips and straightened her posture. "Would you rather I continue to mope and wait for something that will never happen? How many years of my life should I waste?"

He knew she was right. Lexi never ceased to amaze him with her strength and confidence to face challenges, no matter how difficult.

Lexi kissed him on the cheek, grabbed her purse and headed to the front door. Sadie and Stout followed, hoping they were being taken for a ride. Christopher tried to find the words to offer support and guidance as he followed. It troubled him to be failing so miserably. He had been her guardian and protector, but shielding her from heartbreak had proved to be impossible.

"Good luck, Lexi. Call me if you need anything."

"Thanks, Chris. Would you please take Sadie and Stout on a walk for me today? And do not tell Jason that I am coming. I mean it."

Grabbing the pups' collars, Chris nodded.

"All right. See you soon," she said, smiling, before walking to the Jeep.

"This is going to be a long drive," she whispered as she warmed up the engine. She thought intently about needing nerves of steel and the strength of a freight train.

Six hours later, Lexi merged into the heavy Seattle traffic. Rain drizzled, keeping her windshield wipers busy, reminding her that she needed new ones. Horns honked behind her, and brake lights flashed in the stop-and-go traffic. She turned on the defroster and wiped off the inside of the windshield with her hand. After she opened the window slightly, the glass began to clear, allowing her better visibility. She spotted the gondola wheel at the pier and smiled. The lights sparkled as it went around. It was a busy day for ferryboats, setting off to Bainbridge and Bremerton.

Glancing at her phone to check the GPS, she saw that she still had twenty minutes to go. Butterflies were building in her stomach. As she held the steering wheel tight, her thoughts began to play tricks on her. Maybe showing up unannounced wasn't the best idea. Catching him off guard could be bad. *What if he has a woman with him? Oh no.*

"Snap out of it, Lexi. There is no turning back now."

After turning several corners, she came to his street, driving slowly to search for his rental. After spotting his Ford F-150 in the driveway of a small modern-style home, she parked along the curb. Sitting in her Jeep, she watched for any signs of him, knowing it was a subconscious act of stalling. Her legs felt frozen.

"Here goes nothing," she said, hopping out of the Jeep.

A light mist touched her face, reviving her senses. She wrapped her sweater more securely around her and folded her arms to hold it in place. The sea breeze blew her hair off her shoulders and away from her face. Her cheeks tingled as she knocked on the front door. Shivering from nerves, she waited for an answer. Her breath blew out fog as her body bounced to shake the jitters out of her. She decided to try the doorbell, wondering why she hadn't done that in the first place.

No answer. She cupped her hands around her eyes to peek inside the window. No lights were on, no evidence of life at all.

I did not drive this far to give up now.

She walked to the side of the house and opened a small gate leading to the back. Her fingers ran across a vine covering the fence that separated the homes. The green grass squished with each step. Lexi looked down at her black boots, noting small patches of mud and treading carefully not to step into one. A flagstone path leading to the patio caught her attention, and she spotted Jason resting in a hammock supported by a pergola. One leg draped over the side while his hand lay on his stomach. He pushed with his foot to make the hammock sway. He wore jeans, a black thermal shirt and a black ball cap. She couldn't remember the last time she had seen him in a hat. He seemed so content and peaceful. Carefully walking toward him, she looked around to make sure they were alone.

"Hello, Jason."

She moved in closer, picking at her fingernails as she waited for his response.

"Jason?"

He turned his head and stood up from the hammock. Lexi jumped in shock, the fear causing her to gasp.

"Gage?" she said, stepping away from him. "What are you doing here? Why aren't you in jail?"

"Hello, Alexis. I figured you would show up here sooner or later."

He smiled, moving toward her in a calm, cool and collected way. A true sociopath.

"I have been out of jail for some time. Bail and a good lawyer do wonders."

"Do not come any closer, Gage. Where is Jason? Tell me now!"

"I would be more than happy to take you to Jason. Follow me. I would love nothing more than to reunite the two of you."

He gestured toward the inside of the house. She was hesitant to fall for his trap, but she wanted to find Jason.

"I will follow you," she said, eyes narrowing at him.

After Gage walked through the back door of the house, he paused to keep track of Lexi. She followed, her heart pounding and her body trembling.

"Where is he, Gage?"

He ignored her question, leading her to the back of the house. Her eyes roamed, taking in as much detail as possible. No signs of blood or damage to the home. Everything appeared perfectly in place. It looked like a home someone had abandoned. Minimal furniture, no imagination. Gage stopped, grabbing the handle of the bedroom door.

"I have been waiting for this moment, Alexis."

Tears poured nonstop from her eyes as she stared at his hand, terrified at what she would find when he opened the door. He turned the handle, but the door didn't move. Humidity had warped the door, causing it to stick. She shoved Gage aside and used both hands to push the stubborn door open. A large rug lay rolled up in the middle of the room, a large bulge in the middle.

Lexi dropped to her knees, covered her face with her hands and cried uncontrollably. Gage observed with pleasure, feeling victorious.

"Let me see him," she said. "Unroll the carpet ... I want to see for myself."

Gage smiled. "Gladly."

Lexi stood, wiping the tears from her eyes. She watched as he rolled the carpet open. Anger and disgust took over her being. She saw droplets of blood, the size of the soil expanding with each turn. An arm popped out, flopping lifelessly onto the floor.

"Stop!" she yelled.

Gage felt pleased by the look of terror in her eyes. He stood to hover, watching her suffer. Lexi bent down to pick up Jason's hand and then reached inside her boot and pulled out her Glock. She looked at Gage's face as she shot two bullets into his chest.

Boom ... Boom

CHAPTER SIXTEEN

The Discovery

Lexi's body catapulted upward in a violent rush. She fought to control her breathing as she spoke in a panic.

"Jason, Jason!"

Jason grabbed hold of her arms, looking directly into her eyes. "Lexi, I am right here. Baby, it's okay. I'm here. Shhh."

She wrapped her arms around him, trembling with fear. "I dreamt you were, you were ... dead."

He held on to her tightly. "It was just a dream, Lexi. Just a dream. Everything is fine."

"I went to Seattle to bring you home, but Gage was there instead. He killed you. And then I killed him. I'm a murderer."

Jason rubbed her back, kissing the side of her temple. "Gage is locked up for a long time. We won't be seeing him again. We are safe. I promise, Lexi."

He could feel that she was covered in sweat. After retrieving a towel from the bathroom, he handed it to her. She wiped her face, pausing to shed more tears into it.

"It felt so real. I can still hear the ringing in my ears from the gunshots."

"Jeez, Lexi. How about you lay back down? This stress—it is not good for you."

He turned out the light and lay down next to her. His hand came down to rest on her belly bump. He thought about the months he'd been gone ... the things he didn't know. If it hadn't been for Lexi's letter, he may still have been selfishly sulking back in Seattle. She never mentioned a word about her condition. Simply gave him the time and space he asked for. He felt ashamed for leaving her and staying away as long as he did. Lexi knew he would come home immediately if he found out about the pregnancy. Instead, she kept quiet, allowing him the time to heal and find his way back to her. The letter had been a soft nudge. What he really deserved was a slap across the face. It pained him to think about how alone she must have felt during his absence. The secret she kept, dying to get out. Until ultimately, the secret presented itself.

* * *

Lexi walked out to the back shed and dragged out a rake and a box of black trash bags. As a kid, seeing those particular bags sitting beside the shed was a dreaded sign. Every fall, she and Christopher were responsible for yard cleanup. One of the things they learned was the importance of picking the right day to rake. She smiled, remembering the handful of times they spent chasing leaves from the wind instead of containing them. Even now, if wind wasn't the culprit, it was Sadie and Stout. They were like children who, when you weren't looking, would tread through the leaves. Back to square one. Truth was, she enjoyed the exercise and the scenery. The crisp air was refreshing, and the multicolored leaves inspired her senses. Meditation and spirituality all wrapped into one.

Beginning to feel a bit fatigued, she wiped the back of her hand across her forehead. From the corner of her eye, she spotted Christopher heading her way.

"Perfect timing. You can hold the bags while I scoop."

Christopher bent down to grab a trash bag, quiet and sullen.

"Hey. What's up with you?" she asked.

He shook out the bag, using both arms to spread it wide open.

"Did you have a spat with Sutton? What did you do?" Lexi teased.

Christopher didn't crack a smile. Trying to find the words to speak, he looked at her with worry. "Lexi, when are you going to tell Jason?"

"Tell him what exactly?"

"Come on. You're pregnant, Lexi. He doesn't know, does he?"

Lexi held on tight to the handle of the rake as she shifted nervously from one leg to the other.

"I know that you are, Lexi. You have been hiding it pretty well, but all of the signs are there."

"Okay. Yes, I'm pregnant."

Christopher folded his arms wondering what she was thinking.

"Don't look at me like that, Chris. I'm not telling Jason. I can't. He will come home because I'm pregnant. This is the last thing he needs right now. He can make better decisions if he doesn't know."

A look of disapproval emerged on her brother's face.

"Promise me you won't tell him. Promise me, Chris."

"Lexi, what if he decides to stay in Seattle?"

She dropped the rake and placed her hand over her stomach. "Then that is what he will do. I will not have the pregnancy influence his decisions. If he finds out about my condition, he will do what he feels obligated to do. I can't have that."

"Lexi."

"I will tell him ... eventually. Now is not the time. Do you understand that?"

Christopher threw his hands up in defeat. "All right. This is your decision, not mine. Let's finish this yardwork."

He bent down and began shuffling leaves into the bag. Lexi picked up the rake, staring at Christopher's back. She wanted, more than anything, to tell Jason. Telling him now would feel like a trap, a manipulation. Christopher tied the strings to the last garbage bag and hauled the bags to the back of his truck. Lexi followed, wishing his mood didn't reflect judgment.

"Thanks for the help, Chris. I can ride along to the dump with you."

Christopher hesitated before climbing into the truck. "That's okay, Lexi. A drive by myself sounds pretty nice. Think I will stop by and see Sutton while I'm out. Listen, the more time that goes by, the more you are going to show. Jason shouldn't hear about it from someone else. Small town—news travels fast."

"I know, Chris. I will handle this." Lexi touched his arm in reassurance.

She waved as he pulled out of the drive and took off down the road. He was unhappy with her decisions. It left her feeling as though she had disappointed him, and it stung like a whip to the rear. Rubbing her butt with her hand as if she actually felt the burn, she turned to head back inside the house. The day's chores and emotional ups and downs caught up to her. Feeling lightheaded, she went straight to the kitchen for a glass of water. She felt flush and picked up a magazine from the table to fan herself.

"I need to sit down. Must be the joys of pregnancy."

She glanced at the package of chicken thawing on the kitchen counter. Turning up her nose, she stroked her belly as nausea set in. Instead of sitting down, she ran for her bathroom. Before she knew it, she was on her knees, head over the porcelain bowl. Sadie and Stout sat next to her, making the bathroom feel as if it were closing in on her.

She looked at Sadie. "I thought this was just supposed to be a morning thing."

After she vomited all that could possibly have been left in her stomach, the dry heaves set in.

"Come on. Give me a break here," she moaned.

She felt weak and her stomach ached. A man's voice sounded from behind her.

"Lexi? Are you okay?"

She slowly turned her head to find Jason standing in the doorway of the bathroom. He was a sight for sore eyes. Her knight in shining armor.

"Jason."

He stepped closer and bent down to touch her elbow. "Lexi. You're sick."

Her heart warmed as she saw the look of concern in his eyes. She tried to stand up, but her body resisted.

"Here. Let me help you. Let's get you to the bed."

Jason held on securely to Lexi as she tried to stand.

"That's it. There we go."

"Jason, I need some water."

She picked up a glass near the sink, filled it and sipped slowly. Rinsing out her mouth had never felt better.

"Did you catch a bug, Lexi?"

Clearing her throat, she smiled facetiously. "You could say that. Something like a bug."

His brows furrowed inward. "Maybe you should go lay down."

"No. Jason, you are home. I'm so happy to see you. I want to know how you are doing."

"We aren't going to catch up in the bathroom are we?"

Lexi laughed, thankful that things weren't weird between them.

She sat on her bed and maneuvered herself so that she could lean against the headboard. Jason sat beside her, his long legs draped over the side.

"Lexi, your letter—"

A commotion rumbled throughout the house, distracting him.

"Jason!"

Christopher charged into Lexi's room to see his long-lost buddy.

Jason stood to give his friend a hug.

"Hey, man. Good to see you."

"Thanks, Christopher. I got here to find this one sicker than a dog. How long has she been like this?"

Christopher looked at Lexi, unsure what to say. She shook her head discreetly, sending an SOS for him not to spill the beans.

"Um, well. How long? ... Let's see. I haven't really kept track. Just been on her to take care of herself. You know how stubborn she is. Listen to me rambling on. I will leave the two of you to catch up. It is good to have you home, Jason."

Christopher left the room, glaring at Lexi on his way out. Message read loud and clear. He wanted her to tell Jason about the pregnancy.

"What's up with him? He's acting a little strange." Jason's gut told him something was up.

"Christopher has a girlfriend. He has been mysterious and preoccupied for weeks."

Jason sat back down next to her. "No way. I have missed a lot. What is she like?"

"Well, she's nice, very pretty. She is a forest ranger. Right up Christopher's alley. He didn't tell me about her for several weeks."

"That sly dog. Wow. Good for him. It's serious then?"

Lexi smiled. "Definitely serious."

Jason looked down at his hands. Frowning, he thought about all he'd missed over the last several months.

"I'm sorry I have been away so long. Your letter ... it really got to me. Woke me up about a lot of things."

Lexi listened, hanging on every word. She felt anxious. Something inside her warned there was more to the story. Much more.

"I went to Seattle to sort out all of the horrible events from my system. The new job really helped. It kept me distracted and focused on positive things." He rubbed his hands together, pausing to gather more thoughts. "Right after I received your letter, I was offered a promotion. If I agree to take it, I will relocate to Vancouver for a while. The pay is generous and the experience would be amazing."

Lexi crossed her arms over her stomach, her expression deadpan as she listened. The ultimate question ran circles through her mind. She couldn't bring herself to ask. The whole point of the last few months was not to pressure him. Jason placed his hand on her leg.

"Have you decided what you are going to do?" she said.

"I don't feel like I can pass this up. This is the time in my life to embrace an opportunity like this. I am young, with no heavy responsibilities." He smiled, looking into her eyes for a response.

"Jason, I ... Oh, God. I am going to be sick again."

She bolted off the bed and back into the bathroom, closing the door behind her and locking it. Jason walked to the door.

"Lexi, can I do anything for you?"

Tears poured down her face. She used the wall to support her back as she slid to the floor. Her head between her legs, she did everything she could to keep him from hearing her cry.

"Lexi?"

"I just need some time in here, Jason. I will be fine. Go see Christopher."

Jason hesitated to leave her. His hand rested on the door as he pondered what to do. "I will get you some ginger ale."

The thought of the sweet liquid made her gag, but she would agree to anything right now to get him out of her room. Better yet, out of the house.

"You will have to go to the store."

"I will be back in a few, Lexi."

Jason discovered that Christopher had parked behind his truck, blocking him in the driveway. He grabbed the keys to Lexi's Jeep from the hook by the front door and headed out to make a grocery run. After climbing in, he paused to put the seat back. As he turned back to see if the road was clear, he noticed a book sitting on the backseat. He slammed the brakes, put the Jeep in "park" and picked up the book. After staring at it in shock, he fumbled through the pages. *There is only one reason she would have a book like this.* Even he knew that *What to Expect When You're Expecting* was the popular choice for women who were pregnant. He felt a surge build.

"This is why she is sick," he whispered. "Why didn't she tell me?"

He felt angry, confused and ultimately guilty. Lexi had been carrying this burden alone. A combination of fear and happiness overwhelmed his system. Jason loved Lexi. This was good news, surrounded by a secret. He felt betrayed, for it seemed she didn't plan on telling him. And what about Christopher? How long had he known? He rubbed his hand over his face. He had been working up to inviting Lexi to join him in Vancouver when Christopher barreled in and she ran off to the bathroom. He'd come back to Bend for her. Shoving his emotions aside, he derived a plan of his own. He would play along with her secret, making quite certain he was in control of the outcome.

Jason stayed at the Taylor house for several days, pretending to be oblivious to Lexi's condition. He anxiously awaited the weekend's arrival, his own secret on the verge of unfolding. Saturday morning finally rolled around, presenting a sunny, beautiful day. He joined Lexi on the patio, sitting next her on the porch swing.

"I think we should have a picnic at the pond today," he said. "It is a little chilly, but you can layer up. What do you say?"

Lexi sat quietly, contemplating what to do. Until recently, spending time with Jason was all she cared about. Now she wished he would leave. Get on with his life so she could heal her heart and prepare for the baby.

Jason turned to face her. "Lexi?"

"I don't know, Jason. I have a lot to do today. When did you say you were leaving for Vancouver?"

The question felt prickly, but he wasn't having it. He knew what was going through her mind. "I would really like to spend some time with you. Like old times, you know? It won't be long before we see a blanket of snow everywhere. We should take advantage of this beautiful day, Lexi Jane."

Damn, she thought. There would be no getting out of this. She wanted to hide until he left.

"All right, Jason."

"Great. I will take care of everything. You still seem tired from your bout with the flu. I've got this." He was feeling pleased with himself.

"Fine. I will be ready by eleven thirty."

Lexi glanced back and forth at the clothes in her closet. She had been wearing bulky sweatshirts to hide the small bump forming in her stomach. She began to worry. If Jason didn't leave soon, he would discover her secret.

She picked out a navy blue shift dress and paired it with dark gray leggings. Crossing her fingers, she hoped the dress still had enough room to flow over her belly without exposing the bump. She grabbed a pair of brown boots, slipped them on and took one last look at herself in the full-length mirror. Satisfied with her choice, she headed for the kitchen to meet

Jason. Wearing dark blue jeans and a cream-colored wool sweater that zipped partway, exposing a white-collared shirt, he stood leaning against the counter. She stared, admiring his handsome masculinity. As she looked around the kitchen, confusion set in.

"Where is our lunch?"

"Oh, I already took a load down while you were getting ready. I have everything all set up for us."

She squinted at him curiously. There couldn't have been that much stuff. She grabbed her long gray and white sweater. Jason stood behind her to help her put it on.

"All right. Shall we?"

Lexi called Sadie and Stout to follow as they walked the trail to Mirror Pond. The pups took off ahead and stopped to mark every tree. Jason grabbed her hand, slipping his fingers through hers. Caught off guard, she was surprised by the intimate gesture. Ever since he'd come home, things had been friendly but casual. As they got closer to the pond, Lexi could see people from afar.

"Looks like a busy day at the pond. We won't be dining alone."

Jason remained quiet, smiling as he bit his tongue.

"Wait a minute. That is Christopher and Sutton. Did you invite them to join us?"

When they reached the edge of the pond, Lexi let go of Jason's hand to get a closer look at the scene before her. White candles in black lanterns lined both sides of the dock. Two flower pots with green vines and small white flowers flanked the end of the dock. White rose petals lay sprinkled on the planks. She turned to look at him.

"What is going on, Jason?"

He grabbed her hands and looked into her eyes. Her stomach swirled with butterflies as she waited.

"Lexi Jane, I came back to Bend for you. To start a new beginning. I have relieved the demons from my past. Thanks to your love and patience, I am a healthier, happier person. Whatever happens moving forward, I don't want to do any of it without you. Please, marry me today and be my soul mate from this day on."

Tears pooled in her eyes, threatening to overflow. She looked around the pond, noticing that more people had arrived. Olivia stood next to Dr. Stephenson, already a blubbering mess. Lexi looked at Jason, wondering if he knew about the baby.

"Wait. Did Christopher say something to you, Jason? Is that what this is about?"

Jason stroked her shoulders. "I want to marry you, Lexi. That is what's happening here. I know your secret. It wasn't Chris. I found your book. You should have told me. I think I know why you didn't. More importantly, I made my decisions before I knew about the baby. I am truly sorry you had to go through this, wondering if you would end up alone. I'm here for you now and always. You can trust me, Lexi. I promise. I love you."

"We can't—"

"Everything is ready to go, Lexi. You sign a few papers and we are set. We aren't leaving here until I hear the words *Mr. and Mrs. Walker.*"

Sadie and Stout danced around them, smiling from ear to ear the way dogs do. Lexi laughed, wiping the tears from her cheeks. She stepped into Jason's embrace. His mouth took hers, locking on with urgency.

"Come on, Lexi. Everyone is waiting."

He took her hand, leading her to the end of the dock. Christopher stood by Jason, Sadie and Stout sat by Lexi. Friends looked on to witness an event that had been in the making for many years.

CHAPTER SEVENTEEN

Good-bye, Mirror Pond

Jason smiled at the memory of coming home to discover he would be a father. He carefully rolled over to lie on top of Lexi. He stroked the top of her head as he gazed into her eyes, her lashes still wet from crying. The dream had startled her. He worried that the memories of Billy Walker would continue to haunt her.

"I love you, Lexi Jane," he whispered.

His mouth came down on hers. The gesture, so sensual and genuine, left her wanting more. They kissed until a pause for air was necessary. Her hands ravished his body with need.

"I don't want to hurt you," he said. "Am I too heavy?"

"You won't hurt us," she said, smiling devilishly.

He slipped her panties down her legs and over her feet and tossed them into the air. He turned Lexi on her side, lay down behind her and gently entered her. She held on to his leg as his shaft moved in and out of her sweet flesh. He smiled as he felt the curve from the top of her stomach to the bottom with his hand. She felt beautiful. A life growing inside her ... the one they made together. He reached for her breast, trying to be gentle due to the tenderness. They felt fuller, her body preparing for the baby.

"Does that feel okay?"

"Mmm-hmm," she moaned. "Don't stop."

Jason pulled her hair back to kiss the side of her neck, the movement of his shaft never faltering. Lexi held on tighter to his leg, pushing against him deeper. She was wet with need, creating a well-lubricated vessel for their desires. Jason slipped his hand lower, his fingers massaging her clit. Her breathing increased as she pulsed with pleasure. Her orgasm heightened his excitement, pushing him over the edge.

He held her close as they both settled into bliss. They fell into a deep sleep, demons vanquished for the night.

The next day, Lexi and Jason packed for their move to Vancouver. She was excited about their next endeavor, all the while feeling emotional about leaving her home and Christopher. Jason stood in the doorway to her room, watching intently. She sat on her bed clutching a framed picture in her arms. He slowly strolled into the room and sat next to her.

"What have you got there?" he asked, pointing to the picture.

She pulled it away from her chest to show him a photo of her parents.

"I remember that day. Your dad barbecued for all of us. Oh, man, and your mom's mac 'n' cheese. That was a great day. I think you were about twelve years old then?"

"It was my birthday, remember? I wanted a family day BBQ. They always made things special for us."

"Lexi, we can come back to Bend as soon as this job is done in Vancouver."

"I know. My hormones are a mess. Just feeling sentimental and emotional. I will be fine. Besides, maybe Sutton will move in with Christopher. I would love that for him."

Jason rubbed her back, smiling with relief. The last thing he wanted to do was drag Lexi away from a life that meant so much to her. A lifetime of memories.

"We should leave in the morning, try to get an early start," he said.

"Okay. I will be ready."

She stood and wrapped the framed picture inside one of her bulky sweaters to protect it for the move.

"Christopher and I are going to get some more boxes," Jason said. "We are taking the dogs with us."

Lexi smiled, waving as he left. She pulled her clothes out of the closet, deciding to leave the hangers on. A black cozy hoodie caught her eye. She removed it from the hanger and pulled it over her head for warmth. One last walk to Mirror Pond was in order. She went out the back door, down the steps and off through the forest. As she took her time, her mind flooded with visions of her many adventures. She looked forward to the day when her own children would romp around this forest, making their own memories. Would they find love within the surroundings of this magical place like her and Jason did?

She stepped onto the dock and walked to the end. The air was still, cold and crisp. She wrapped her arms around her shoulders as a shiver ran through her body. The water looked like pure glass as she appreciated her reflection bouncing off of it. Her lips curved into a smile. She closed her eyes, seeing images in her mind of fishing with the boys, swimming in the pond and chasing them through the forest.

When her eyes opened, she became startled when another person's reflection appeared beside hers on the water, causing her smile to falter and her heart to race with concern. Before she could turn around to see who was lurking behind, someone grabbed her and placed their hand over her mouth. Lexi squirmed and jerked to get away, fear and panic making it difficult to think. The grip around her waist got tighter and tighter. Darkness became all that she could see. Silence, the only presence that lingered in the air and the reflections at Mirror Pond disappeared.

"In our own mirror, we can see the truth of the soul"
– Andy Fox

THE END

If you enjoyed this book, look for the author's
previous romance novel, Mason's Gray.